Paintwork

Tim Maughan

Paintwork

Copyright © 2011 Tim Maughan

Cover design and artwork by Bobi Richardson
Proofing and editing by Jude Clarke

ISBN: 1463570465
ISBN-13: 978-1463570460

Dedicated to Chris Maughan,
for ensuring the house was always full
of computers and science fiction.

Paintwork

3Cube's feet hurt. His limited edition Eugene SureShot Nikes are two sizes two small for him, in order to try and fool the gait-tracking software. It is an old writer trick, one that 4Clover had taught him before he got sent down. Advice from a jailed writer. To be fair though it wasn't the gait-trackers, face-clockers or even the UAVs that got 4Clover in the end. The word on the timelines had said it was a Serbian zombie-swarm hired by an irate art critic that had tracked him down and smeared his co-ordinates all across the Crime and ASB wikis. Right in the middle of a bombing too. Caught red-handed; stencil in one hand, beetle juice in the other.

3Cube doesn't recall 4Clover ever saying anything about the shoes splitting. Stretched too far by his ill-fitting feet, he knows the Nikes are split, because he can feel the Bristol drizzle soaking up into his socks. He can hear the drizzle too, *taptaptaptaptap* on the hood of his Adidas stormsuit. The Adidas isn't too small at least, in fact it's over-sized and saggy in the decades-old writers' style, the one-piece's crotch hanging somewhere between thighs and knees. 3Cube likes the Adidas; it's relatively new, unworn. The thermostat still works, for a start; the vents still opening just in time to stop him from getting too clammy.

Plus he likes the classic three-stripe pattern that runs down the arms and legs. It feels like a badge of writers' honour, that stretches back decades. Tradition, even. It feels like a uniform.

Except after tonight he won't be able to wear it again for at least two months. Another 4Clover trick.

3Cube waits, the 3 a.m. drizzle hanging in the air around him. The light from the occasional passing car on the A4 behind picks up the raindrops for an instant, giving the whole scene more depth. 3Cube thinks about depth a lot. Depth, perspective. How to force and manipulate both. It is what he is best known for, second to being the best QR Code writer in South Bristol.

Take the billboard in front of him right now, for example. It is meticulous, unblemished. The red and white of its generic Coca-Cola design seems to shimmer under its protective nano-gloss. All around it though is chaos; every inch of wall is covered in QR Codes – some on stickers, some stencilled – until their matrix of barcodes has merged together to produce a disorientating mess of black and white pixels, like an ancient building's prized mosaic floor ripped apart by tectonic shifts. 3Cube resists focussing on any single one, instead seeing them as a single, sprawling mass. He doesn't want to trigger a bombing or a throwup, and anyway he put most of them there. He knows where the QR Codes lead – the few that aren't long dead links, at least – and he has no interest in his view being filled with flat flyers for club nights and illicit dark-nets. That's his business, his day job; bombing the streets with digital flyposters, physical links to unreal places. Real paint, paper, glue and beetle juice giving birth to non-existent pixels fleetingly projected onto consenting retinas.

But tonight isn't about the day job. Tonight is about the art.

3Cube waits, knowing soon the signal will come from Tera, his unseen guardian angel. Unseen and never met, he knows he can trust Tera, that somewhere hidden deep in the damp greyness of Bristol's collapsing architecture he sits with the

CopWatch and Antisocial Behaviour wikis open in front of him, his army of spiders monitoring the data and voice bursts. Between the disgruntled pensioners posting the precise loitering patterns of bored teenagers to the legit wikis, and the dealers and look-outs reporting squad car and UAV movements to the illegal ones, he is putting together a real-time model of police activity across South Bristol. 3Cube trusts him not just because Tera is one of the best, but also because the unseen hacker was once a writer himself, and understands how unfortunate it would be for one of those occasional passing cars to light the raindrops in alternating blue and red at just the wrong moment.

He shudders, thinking of 4Clover again. Caught red-handed, right in the middle of a bombing, stencil in one hand, beetle juice in the other.

So he waits for Tera's signal before moving, and as he does he lets his eyes fall onto the billboard's own QR Code, a thirty centimetre square black and white grid, shimmering under the protective nano-gloss. Untouched, unblemished. He focusses on it, and double-blinks acceptance.

The surface of the billboard starts to shimmer and flex. Ripples start to emanate from its centre as a huge can of Coke emerges from its surface, ring-pull end first. It reminds 3Cube of a tube train at first, but then it starts to buck and move, and he realises it's meant to be a rodeo horse. The big clue is the Chinese cowgirl sat astride it, undoubtedly some vurt star 3Cube doesn't recognise, her outfit a focus group-assembled mess of Old West Americana and Asian sci-fi lingerie.

Stars and brightly-lit bubbles fill the air around 3Cube, blocking out the drizzle, while streaks of rainbow light encircle him like a psychedelic lasso. Gently the cowgirl leans forward towards him, her smile simultaneously enchanting and disturbingly vacant, the stars and bubbles reflected in her deep brown eyes. She reaches out an impossibly long and elegant siren's arm, and with a perfectly tanned hand strokes the side of

3Cube's face so gently that for a second he can almost *feel* her.

Then he rips the spex from his face, and she is gone. There is nothing left except for the cold air, the drizzle, the generic red and white Coca-Cola branding.

Just as swiftly, he puts his spex back on; impatient that he might miss Tera's cue. Still the ad in front of him is passive, the girl trapped behind the wall of nano-gloss and beetle juice, waiting for his gaze to fall once again on the QR code. He resists, and waits.

Something chimes behind his left ear, and in the top right of his periphery an icon appears. A cartoon head - goatee beard, baseball cap, lit cigar – winks at him, as a hand appears next to it, thumb raised.

Time to move.

Tera doesn't tell him how long he's got, but 3Cube knows not to fuck around. He drops to one knee on the damp pavement, simultaneously whipping his backpack around to his front. In a series of rehearsed moves his left hand goes into the pack, initially grabbing and unrolling the first stencil. It's of an empty square, perfectly cut to the same size as the billboard's QR code. Then his other hand goes back in the bag, and out comes the aerosol of white beetle juice. His left hand struggles to hold the stencil against the impossibly frictionless nano-gloss surface – the drizzle isn't helping – while the right shakes the can and then directs the spray onto the stencil. Quickly the beetle juice, the only thing 3Cube knows of that will actually stick to the nano-gloss, starts to obliterate the QR code until only a perfectly-formed white square is left.

Then both hands are back in his bag. First out is the second stencil, followed by the aerosol of black beetle juice. The stencil, a seemingly random mess of smaller software-calculated squares, had taken him hours to cut out precisely, and he checks its orientation three times before filling it with black. As the two colours merge the beetle juice fumes fill his nostrils, and 3Cube curses himself for forgetting to bring a facemask;

the chemicals burning his sinuses as he imagines the paint's tiny machines flooding into the blood vessels in his nose. The thought of it, even though he knows he's probably overreacting, creeps him out to the point of near panic.

He momentarily closes his eyes and focusses again. Gently he peels away the second stencil, and allows himself a little smile – the resulting QR code looks perfect, indistinguishable from the billboard's own at first glance. And one glance is all it takes.

3Cube makes sure everything is back in his pack and it's zipped up tight before rising to his feet again. He steps back and blinks acceptance at the freshly painted mass of black and white pixels.

Again the surface of the billboard starts to shimmer and flex, but instead of a gentle ripple the centre of the board blows out backwards, as though someone has punched a hole through a huge sheet of paper. Torn shards billow gently in the wind, and through this ragged portal 3Cube can see the skyline of Bristol, as though he's looking through the billboard, across the sea of warehouses and industrial units towards the seventy year old towers of the Barton Hill Estate that he calls home. 3Cube allows himself another smile It's the first time he's been able to test the depth and perspective he painstakingly calculated from Google Maps and Street View. It looks perfect, almost photorealistic.

But the illusion doesn't stay set for long. After precisely two seconds the sun starts to burst out from the dark clouds above the towers, banishing the drizzle and turning the Bristol night sky to day. The view turns from monochrome to electric, vivid colour; and where the sunlight - so warm-looking he can almost *feel* it - hits the structures below they start to transform, huge exotic-looking plants and flowers erupting from the postwar industrial landscape, until the whole scene has become fields of organic, inviting nature. Behind them the towers are warping, becoming more colourful too, as their geometry takes on a thick, felt-pen-scribbled style. The whole thing looks like a child's drawing brought to vivid, three-dimensional life.

3Cube's smile spreads into a satisfied grin.

Something buzzes angrily behind his left ear, and in the top right of his periphery the icon turns red. The cartoon head looks worried, and the hand next to it flips upside down, thumb pointing to the ground.

Time to move.

*

3Cube thumbs off the cheap IKEA mirror in his mum's bathroom as he brushes his teeth. He doesn't want to see any of his timelines, or any of the street-art feeds that the mirror so thoughtfully serves up for him whenever it recognises his face. Instead he is left gazing at a smudged thumbprint pressed in toothpaste and saliva, and his own slightly gaunt face. He looks tired. But then he's hardly slept, buzzing too much from the excitement.

He is the same every time he drops a major piece. Lying in bed waiting for dawn, and then forcing himself to wait that hour or so longer until the commuter traffic has kicked in. He avoids the feeds and online chatter until he's gone and seen it himself; the looks on the passers-by as they see it for the first time. This is street art and his real audience is the street: the commuters and the office girls, the tramps and the scruffy school kids. If all he wanted was the views of the graf-hipsters and the art bloggers then he could just dump the URL online and let them all pile in. It will happen soon enough anyway, in fact it's probably already started - it only takes one early morning wanderer, starting an early shift or skulking back from a club, to have grabbed it for their timeline for it to be all over the art-wikis. Which is why 3Cube always maintains radio silence until he's gone down and seen it himself. He'll take a first hand wry smile or a confused glance over the re-posted echoes of a gushing thousand-word review or a sarcastic hundred and forty-character tweet any time. He leans to spit down the sink, and catches sight of himself in the mirror again. His reflection is already looking more awake, grinning back at him with a wry smile.

Time to move.

*

It is 8.37 am on a Wednesday morning when the bus dumps 3Cube into the mass of commuters emptying out of Temple Meads Station. He's wearing a different storm suit, a red and white Puma number, and this morning his matching trainers actually fit his feet.

As he crosses the bridge onto the A4 his heart starts to thump in his chest, his mouth dry with anticipation. His spex are still in his pocket, but he doesn't need the timelines to tell him how his burn has been received.

There's a small group – maybe eight or nine people that he can see from this distance – stood around the billboard, gazing at it. Actually stood there. Not passing it, not glancing at it: actually stood looking at it. An audience of people who have stopped of their own accord to admire it. Like it was an actual piece of art.

He stops in his tracks observing the scene, giddy with satisfaction and relief. There are seven people now - a couple have drifted away - but as he watches another stops. A young woman, maybe twenty one years old. Unlike the rest of the group, which looks to be mainly made up of students or graf-heads drawn down to check out the timeline buzz, she's dressed in thigh-high transparent boots that stop just an inch short of a smartly tailored but cheap looking storm jacket. Standard office wear this season, and 3Cube guesses she probably works for one of the ad-hoc trend speculation firms based in Temple Quay. A short-term temp with no long term plans, and more interest in the Shanghai gossip timelines than the memetic trend ones she's paid to blankly follow for eight hours a day.

Watching her, 3Cube feels another victorious relief flood over him. One Bristol office-girl, stopped in the street to admire his work, is worth a terabit of global timeline-chatter bandwidth to him; it proves he can do it, push his work to the next level, from outside his follower-sphere and across to the mainstream. Slowly he starts to move closer to her, watching her face as she flicks a windblown strand of hair away from her scarlet painted lips, and gently pushes her spex up onto her forehead so she can take a better look.

Gently pushes her spex up onto her forehead so she can take a better look.

Wait…what?

3Cube stops dead in his tracks again, glancing quickly at the rest the small crowd, each one in turn. None of them are wearing spex.

From where he's standing he's at a right angle to the actual billboard, and can't see the ad or his QR code. Instinctively he darts across the road, oblivious to the angry beeps of the rush-hour traffic, so he can get a clear view.

It looks like a hole has blown through the billboard, revealing the vista behind. The same vista he had so meticulously created, but with all the vibrancy gone. All the colour. The blue sky is now the purest of pitch black, the warm sun replaced by a rain of fin-tailed bombs, each one emblazoned with the Coca-Cola logo. Fizzy-drink can bombs, raining down onto the decaying, crumbling towers of Barton Hill that now look somehow both detailed and faded, like an image from an old school textbook that's been photocopied one too many times. Along their base runs a field of flowers, shrivelled and dying, falling away into nothing but black and white splatter against the corporate red background, as if the impervious nano-gloss has been burned and eaten away by some hazardous, industrial acid. It looks like someone has taken 3Cube's piece and sucked all the naïve positivity and rebellion out of it, replacing it with bold, stark anger and nihilism. It is also – perhaps most strikingly - firmly, proudly two-dimensional.

Someone has bombed the whole billboard, with actual paint.

Well, with beetle juice, of course. And lots of it. In the only two, utterly unmixable, colours the street has ever seen. It's a huge piece, chaotic yet precisely realised. And it's a clear diss at his work too; a blatant, insulting go-over. It's a declaration of war. From whom he can't yet tell; there's a signature, but it's written in indecipherable wild-style hieroglyphs.

Right across his perfectly crafted, and now so effectively destroyed, QR code.

3Cube is frozen to the spot, numb, when a dirty looking minivan with an animated JCDecaux logo on its side pulls up to the kerb in front of him. He knows the logo all too well - every writer does - because it sits below every billboard in the city. Out of the driver's seat struggles a fat little balding man in a hi-vis storm suit, day-glo orange with scruffy silver details. He mutters under his breath as he walks over to stand next to 3Cube. Facing the billboard he pulls goggles down over his eyes as he raises an input-gloved hand to waist height and starts to air-type.

Usernames and passwords, 3Cube guesses. He's seen this happen before, too many times. Every time, in fact. From over the lip of the top of the billboard a nightmarish shape appears, a mess of too many insect limbs and a vibrating plastic carapace. The billboard's beetle, awakened from its secure nest. Slowly, but disturbingly naturally, the little robot works its way down the expanse of nano-gloss, on feet somehow capable of clinging to the frictionless surface. 3Cube expects it to stop as it reaches the paintwork, but of course it keeps on going. On a day like today, he thinks, there can be only one thing it is interested in, as it continues its horrific crawling descent to where his already near-obliterated QR code sits.

It waits for a second, until the little man from JCDecaux air-types some more commands. And then, with the sort of machine precision that reminds him he isn't watching an insect or another artist, it starts to spray short bursts of beetle juice from where its mandibles should be, white and black, gradually recreating the original ad's QR code.

His work is gone. The signature is gone. But the anonymous signatory's art still remains, as bold and stark as ever.

As if to answer his train of thought, the little orange and silver man speaks.

"I can't blat the whole thing out, not enough juice left. Plus it'd take fucking hours." he says. "I don't know, people round here just don't care, do they? Don't understand money, that's the thing. Probably because they never bloody seen any, to be fair. But they don't understand. Every time they do something like this they're costing someone money."

He sighs and looks back at the billboard, the beetle still labouring away like a mutated, organic inkjet printer. "I dunno, I see a lot of shit sprayed up around here. Most of it nonsense or AR links. But don't see much like this. Looks a bit dated to me…but…" He trails off, and looks back at 3Cube. "You look like you know about this stuff – is that any good?"

"Yeah." Says 3Cube, his mouth dry. "Yeah, it is."

*

3Cube hurls a mug right through Tera's avatar's face, splattering cold tea over the faded Leo Kim poster above his bed.

"Just calm the fuck down man." the avi says, peering out at him from under its cartoon baseball cap as it hovers cross-legged in the corner of his room. "I know what you must be thinking, but I swear-down it's fuck-all to do with me."

"Bullshit." 3Cube hollers back at him, ignoring his mum's shouts from the next room to keep the noise down. "You set up the hosting for my burn, you knew exactly where I was go-

14

ing to drop it, you were watching the feeds. Who the fuck else could it have been?"

"I dunno 'Cube, all I can say is- "

"Don't talk to me like I'm fucking retarded. Don't fucking lie to me. That paint-over is a direct fucking diss- "

"That doesn't prove anything- " Tera is cut short by an ashtray sailing through his forehead.

"FUCK YOU!" screams 3Cube. "Fuck you! No one had seen my burn apart from you!"

"Just calm the fuck down 'Cube man! Shut the fuck up and think about this!" Tera's avi scratches its head through its non-existent baseball cap. "Have you even checked the timelines yet? For all you know someone might have walked past five minutes after you'd finished and posted it all across the fucking net, and it'd be sitting there just waiting for someone to take a pop."

"Nah." 3Cube replies, doubtful but starting to mellow. "They would have had to have got their shit together too quickly. Too much of a fucking coincidence."

"Is it though?" Tera protests. "Is it really? Think about it. How many haters you got following you man? How many people biting on your style? How many wannabe writers with alerts set up to track your every move, so they can be the first person to take a shot at the legendary 3Cube?"

'I dunno…"

"Really fam, think about it. There's a lot of petty fuckers out there, you know that better than me."

He has a point, but 3Cube still isn't convinced.

"Look, I can see you're vexed," the avi continues, "But I swear to you I had fuck all to do with this. And I can prove it. Just come visit me at my place, and I'll prove to you I didn't do it. That it couldn't have been me."

"Serious?" 3Cube is surprised. Hackers like Tera never meet anyone they work with in person, let alone casually invite them round to their mysterious top-secret lairs.

A spinning sphere blinks into existence in the top right corner of 3Cube's view, a Google Maps link.

"Serious." replies Tera, his avatar trying its hip-hop cartoon best to portray sincerity. "Come over now, we'll get all this sorted. I promise you."

*

3Cube vaguely remembers a teacher at his school explaining the history of Bristol harbour to a restless class, about how when it was built it had been a wonder of modern engineering. Two hundred years later it was practically deserted, until the city decided to revive it, encouraging businesses and developers to come convert the decaying sheds and warehouses into bars, art centres and luxury flats.

It had worked out for a while, and then - just after 3Cube had been born - the economy had got bad, and no one could afford to eat in the fancy restaurants, let alone live in the even fancier apartments. His teacher had said that most of the people that had lived here had been rich students from the Far East and India, but when the government had decided the universities were a waste of money they'd mainly stopped coming. As a result, most of them had slowly become squats and communes for hippysters, guild members and junkies. Not long after that the droughts and famines had hit North Africa hard, and for the first time in over a century the harbour was filled with boats again, spilling their cargoes of hungry refugees out into the empty buildings.

Which was why for a long while, when 3Cube was still a kid, he was too scared to come down here. The adults told you not to for a start, as "those foreigners were so hungry they might put you in a pot". For a year or two it had even been fenced off while everyone inside had been 'processed', and no-one could get in or out without having their retinas scanned by the bouncers on the gates. Then there had been some protests and some riots, and they'd torn down the fences, and everything had changed again - the refugees and the hippysters had started to re-open the bars and clubs, and put on raves and parties in the warehouses. Suddenly instead of it being a place 3Cube and his friends were scared of it was somewhere they obsessed over, a world of loud music and bright lights shimmering on the water, of crowded walkways and smiling, shouting people - an escape from the oppressive, greying towers of the estates they awoke to every day.

But today 3Cube can feel a little of that child's fear return. It is barely 11am but already the harbour side is busy with bodies, the smell of African spices and fried meats from the food stalls filling the air. He's not eaten properly today, but he's not even hungry. He's too angry, and uncomfortable about Tera asking him to come here to meet him. His head is full of those net myths about hackers downloading genome maps and building custom viruses to infect people that piss them off, and even though he knows it's probably all bullshit he's decided he's not going to eat or drink anything until he's got home and had a shower.

He's following a trail of indigo footprints floating an inch above the pavement, put there by his spex based on what Google Maps thinks is the best route. He pauses as the crowds thin out and he sees the footprints disappear into the entrance hall of some squats that were once luxury executive apartments, but now ooze bass rumbles and the smell of stewing genetically modified, harbour-grown seaweed. Maybe Tera gave him a fake link. Maybe he hacked Google Maps, or his spex. Maybe he's about to walk into a Libyan chem factory full of angry blaze-heads. Or maybe he's just being paranoid.

He adjusts the collar on his stormsuit and glances behind him, trying to shake off the fear, before following the footprints again.

*

Twenty minutes later 3Cube is sitting in Tera's small room, quietly sipping on a mug of strong tea, any fears of custom-built viruses completely forgotten.

"So," the hacker says to him, grinning curiously, "You're convinced it couldn't have been me now, yeah?"

"Yeah. Of course." 3Cube keeps glancing around the room, his eyes constantly re-scanning the walls that are covered with photos and posters, club flyers and fraying art prints. Despite how much there is, he feels like he's looked at everything a hundred times already, his eyes desperate to find something new.

In reality, they're just desperate to avoid looking at Tera. And those legs.

"What's the matter?" says Tera, tapping the arm of his wheelchair with his mug like he's noticed, "This thing freaking you out?"

"No, no. Of course not."

"Not seen one before?"

"No, of course I have... just, y'know. Not that often."

The thirty-something hacker grins again. For only the second time since he's arrived 3Cube lets himself look at him properly, and instantly feels guilty for feeling awkward. Tera looks uncannily like his avatar, right down to the baseball cap and goatee. The only major differences are he's carrying a few extra pounds - but then who doesn't make their avi a bit slimmer? - and those legs. The completely lifeless, unmoving, awkwardly-angled legs.

"Can't you get them fixed?"

"In theory, yeah. My spinal cord was severed near the base, so a few months of stem-cell insertion and stimulation and it should re-grow itself." Tera shrugs. "Apparently I'm on a waiting list. Have been for at least 12 years now. NHS. Only alternative is to go private, but you wouldn't believe how much that costs. We have the technology, if you have the money. Viva la

18

singularity".

Tera suddenly laughs loudly at this last bit, and 3Cube joins in, even though he doesn't understand it. Must be some kind of hacker joke.

Tera sighs. "I tried one of those exoskeletons for a while, you know like the army vets get? I dunno. It was uncomfortable. Itchy and it got smelly. Needed fucking charging every few hours. Plus.. I dunno. They're a pain to get in and out of. Especially if you're on your own, y'know? So I actually feel more independent in this thing."

3Cube is flushed with guilt again. "I'm sorry man. Really, I- "

"Hey, don't worry about it. I'm not. It's been 12 years, I've got used to it."

*

Tera had told him the story when he'd first arrived. The condensed life story.

At school Tera had loved drawing, sketching, painting. His art teacher heaped praise upon him on a weekly basis, telling him if he worked hard on improving his skill he would be able to walk into the best art schools the nation had to offer, and from there wherever he wanted his career to take him. And work hard he did, devoting every spare moment to honing his talents. His single mum was ecstatic, telling all her friends, and sticking his pictures on the fridge and joking about how she was going to sell them for millions when he was famous.

At around the age of fifteen, like so many kids in Bristol, Terra became absorbed into the city's mesh of street culture. It was the music that caught him first, then the clothes and the attitude, but one thing above all became the centre of his focus: graffiti. He found himself poring over websites and wikis, studying the colourful LA slum murals and bold New York Subway burns until he knew every airbrush stroke. He snuck away on Saturdays with his mum's camera to hunt around Bristol for the latest pieces he'd read about online, or to gaze at the few, still-remaining Banksy works. He practised in his mum's garage, on old bits of corrugated cardboard, until he was confident enough. And then he took it out on the streets.

Over the course of about two years, Tera's pieces start to spring up all over the city, from small tags on bus stops to large, complex works under the ring road's various flyovers. He skulked around the city in the early hours, darting under robotic surveillance cameras with a ninja-like bandanna over his face and a clanking knapsack full of car-repair spray cans on his back, his hands stained with multicoloured rainbows. He was building himself a fierce rep, not just with the city's graf scene, but also its law enforcement agencies. But even that wasn't enough. His passion was bordering on obsession, and he had to try and push it further. He started heading up to London, not just to take pictures, but to paint them.

One night, after he'd been hanging out there for a few months, he was invited to a party in a disused tube station somewhere in the East End. He was wary at first, but the invite itself was a sign that his London rep was building, and he couldn't resist showing his face. When he got there he couldn't believe he'd thought about not going. They had a generator down there, for the lights and the sick sound system that was blaring out hip-hop and dubstep. And of course there was the graffiti. There were about five major pieces in progress, taking shape in front of his eyes over the course of the night, plus people were just spraying shit and tagging anywhere they wanted, chilling and smoking and trading tips. That night he put faces to some of the names whose work he'd admired for years, and they talked graf to him like he was their equal. For once he felt like he had somewhere he was meant to be.

And then the police turned up. Quietly at first. They just seemed to walk in. Everyone just stared at them for a few seconds before someone cut the power, and the lights and beats were replaced by the chaos of flashing torches and barking dogs. Everyone started running, in every direction. In the darkness Tera found himself following some guy he'd been chatting to down into the tunnel, where it was even darker and wet, with rats writhing in the darkness. Torch lights and angry shouts followed them, drowned out only by the thunder of tube trains that sounded far too close and the thumping of Tera's own heart. He fell and tore his jeans, but got up and ran again. Someone else fell but didn't make it up, and then the shouts and lights were further behind; and he paused, exhausted, lying on his front, ready to surrender; until everything lit up like daytime and he felt the wheels of the tube train slice through his back.

He was in hospital for over six weeks, bored and unable to move. It was one of those hospitals in London - an ancient building that stank of sorrow and chemicals - because they couldn't move him to Bristol safely. Which meant his mum, between working and looking after his kid brother, couldn't get up to see him very often. When she did she tried to smile and put on a brave face, but really Tera could see she was just tired and disappointed.

The day he came home she couldn't make it, so they put him in the back of an ambulance on his own, and he sat there for the two hour drive in total silence. When the doors were finally opened and he could see daylight again they were parked outside his mum's place. She was nowhere to be seen. Instead the police were there, on his doorstep, waiting for him.

They were taking every single piece of his art that was in the house, and tossing it into the back of a van. He tried to tell them that some of it was his A-level Art coursework, but they ignored him, telling him it was nothing more than evidence. Exhausted, he wheeled himself into the kitchen, where his distraught mum and confused brother sat sobbing. They had even taken the pictures from the fridge. In fact, they had taken every single piece of paper they even suspected of bearing his handwriting. He didn't even hear them when they finally arrested him, he just stared, in silent shock, at his mum's crumpled, destroyed face as she cried, and let them push him out to the van.

It turned out it had all been an elaborate sting operation; the party organised by a graf artist that had got into a little trouble himself and had turned grass in response. He'd not only given up everyone's name, but also helpfully arranged an occasion where they could all be found under the same roof.

Tera was charged with over two hundred counts of wanton and deliberate vandalism, and got a two grand fine and a month of community service. His mum didn't talk to him for a further six. He never got any of his work back. Which of course meant he would have failed his Art A-level, if he hadn't already dropped out of college. In fact, he told 3Cube, he would never so much as touch a pencil again, as the thought of doing so seemed alien to him now, doing nothing but flood his mind with images of his mum and brother, still crying at the kitchen table.

*

"So what you gonna do now?" asks Tera, his eyes darting about looking at the multitude of windows that surround him. Wiki pages, video streams, timelines, pages of code and what look like complex, ever evolving flow charts. 3Cube has never shared the workspace of a proper hacker before, and he feels kind of privileged, even if he doesn't understand half of what is going on.

"What am I gonna do? I'm gonna drop the next piece tonight. What else can I do?"

Tera momentarily turns away from the translucent, floating walls of data to look 3Cube in the eyes. "Really?"

"Yeah, really. It's a three-night trilogy. I thought about redropping the first piece, but fuck it. No looking back."

"Fair enough. I just wondered if you were going to try and

Time to move.

*

"You okay?" Tera asks. Looking at 3Cube's crumpled face, it's a pretty redundant question.

"Yeah. I'm fucking great."

Tera turns back to the wall of floating windows. A bunch of them are showing timelines and blogs full of images of the paint-over on 3Cube's latest piece; the towers of Barton Hill remodelled into the lifeless fossils of a long dead dinosaur, dead white bones being picked away at by black circling carrion. It's morbid and full of futility, as if declaring with nihilistic glee that Bristol and its decades old street art movement were finally dead, but it's hard not to be moved and impressed by it. Certainly most of the commentators and tweeters are.

"The first grabs starting coming in about 6.30am. So a few hours after you finished. Not that anyone would have bothered taking pics before that, it probably would have been too dark. But no-one walked past and grabbed... whoever in the process. Which is fucking annoying."

"Yeah," 3Cube says, unenthusiastically. "That's what I don't get. It's a big piece. They would have needed a ladder or scaffold. Which means a van. It's pretty exposed along there. They were fucking lucky."

"I dunno. I dunno if luck has anything to do with it. You gotta assume they had someone watching the wikis and shit like I was. Plus you picked that board in the first place because it's in a CCTV blind spot, and there's fuck-all traffic down there at that time of the morning."

"I guess. But... I dunno. It's the scale of it, man. Look at it." 3Cube throws a laser-style pointer onto one of the images with his finger, stretching it out until it its almost a metre across, dominating the air in Tera's little room. "Its clearly a direct response to my piece, and there's some elaborate fucking stencil work there. How the fuck did they get that together so quickly man? How the fuck do you explain that?"

"Whoa" Tera raises his hands in protest "Lets not fucking go there again. I swear to you I don't know- "

"Yeah. Yeah I know. It's nothing to do with you. I believe you. I just don't get it though. How they could have their shit together like that?"

Tera sighs. "Look, like I've said to you before on a hundred runs, this ad-hoc hosting I use isn't perfect. By definition the AR files have to be publicly available, you know that. Now I don't put 'em up till as late as possible, but that's like an hour before the drop, just to avoid DNS issues. And I don't advertise them, naturally. But if people wanted to find them – were really determined to do it – they could. There's some crazy shit you can do with trawl agents these days. You'd be surprised.

"As for the stencils…you cut all yours by hand right? Takes you fucking hours? Kids these days are doing them with fucking 3D printers and fabbers and shit. Just knock up a design at home and the printer churns out the stencil for you, all pre-cut."

"Yeah. I guess you're right." 3Cube feigns appeasement, but in reality what Tera is saying is making him even more uncomfortable. It's partly because he's still not sure if he can trust him, but largely because it chimes perfectly with what Artefackt had said to him. 3D printers. Instant designs. Everything is too easy. Disposable. Copied and deleted. Digital and ephemeral. Easily forgotten.

Apart from the two paint-overs, which are still standing, blatant and unavoidable for anyone passing.

"You gonna do the last piece tonight?" Tera asks him.

"Yeah." He replies. "Of course. What have I got to lose?"

*

"Come in, come in!" Thomas grins toothlessly at him,

beckoning him excitedly with one arm, "Quickly, before anyone sees you! Quickly!"

3Cube steps over the taut string barrier, knocking it with his thigh and triggering the clanking of tin cans and bottles that make up the camp's intruder defences. Thomas' place is completely hidden from the casual passers-by on the A4 - a couple of tarpaulin-covered tents sheltered behind two billboards – unless you can be bothered to pay attention and notice the tell tale signs of protruding poles and guy ropes. Most people can't, 3Cube assumes, judging by how long the old tramp has lived there without being disturbed or moved on.

"Tea? That would be nice." Thomas glances around the muddy, rubbish covered floor as if he's lost something. "Do you want a tea? Hmm? Tea?"

"I'm fine man, thanks."

"Really? No tea? Not a nice cup of tea?"

"No, really Tom. No tea. But thank you." 3Cube always feels guilty when he comes to visit Thomas; they both know he's really only there for one reason, but 3Cube has a soft spot for the old homeless man, built partly from admiration of his fierce independence. Despite the smell of damp cardboard and rotting vegetation it's hard not to be impressed by this tiny, secret world that Thomas has built for himself.

That admiration aside, 3Cube can't come to Thomas' little kingdom without feeling on edge, uncomfortable. Years ago he used to think it was Thomas himself – the kids at school used to whisper that he was a wizard or a kiddie-fiddler or even a cannibal that had escaped from the refugee camps – but slowly 3Cube realised it wasn't the scruffy but harmless old man at all. It was something else, something that usually just dwelled in his dreams, but that right now he could sense was there, shuffling, just out of the corner of his eye, and scratching, just above the dull drone of traffic.

With morbid fascination he finds himself drawn to the cages in the corner of the camp, built from what appears to be a mix of abandoned rabbit hutches and old shopping trolley parts. There are six in total, stacked three levels high, and all but one is occupied.

3Cube moves closer, but not too close.

All along the top of the cages, and dotted around the highest parts of the camp and along the rear side of the billboards themselves, are a variety of receptacles. Upturned plastic drink bottles with the bottoms cut off, pieces of abandoned guttering, funnels like he used in science lessons in school. They are all held in position, pointing towards the sky, with duct tape and nails. From the bottom of each one extend hoses and rubber pipe, a tangled mess of tubing that leads back to the stack of cages.

"It's for the rain" explains Thomas, as he notices 3Cube staring at his elaborate water-collection set-up. "For the rain water. It goes down the holes. Then down the tubes. You see? Down the tubes. Into the cages."

3Cube follows the hosepipe from one of the collectors – this one fashioned from an old cider bottle – and indeed it does lead into one of the cages. He feels his chest tighten as he leans forward to peer into the shadows within.

Something in there looks like it is breathing.

"Usually the board holes are enough, see?" Thomas is pointing at the back of one of the billboards. Along the top, hidden from the public is a strip of guttering, a long plastic tube with holes cut into it. "See? The board holes. That's enough to feed one of 'em. But I got loads here. I've always got loads. So I needs more water you see? Loads more."

In the cage, 3Cube can start to make out a shape. The beetle lies there on a mass of shredded and pulped newspaper, its whole body heaving gently with the pained breathing of an abused, wounded animal. Its twitching carapace is stained with filth and cigarette burns, and one leg is missing, leaving a stump that bleeds wiring and broken servitors. 3Cube can see now that the hosepipe feeds in through a hole on the wooden back of the cage, and connects to where the beetle's mouth should be, held in position with yet more duct tape. The set up reminds him, when coupled with the pained breathing, of old TV images he'd seen of hunger-striking refugees being force-fed. He feels a bit sick.

"They drink it?" he asks.

"No. They don't drink it. Not exactly. No. They make the beetle juice with it. You see? The beetle juice. The rain goes in there, into their bellies. You see? And in there it mixes with the machines. The tiny little machines in their bellies. And that makes the beetle juice. Two colours. You see? They don't drink it. No."

"About the beetle juice, Thomas – you sold much recently? I mean more than usual? To anyone unusual?"

"No. No. No one unusual. Just the usual people. Just the usual."

"Yeah, but is anyone buying large amounts, Thomas? I mean a lot? Is anyone wanting to buy a lot of beetle juice from you?"

"No. No." The old hobo looks at the ground, scratches his beard, agitated. He's clearly nervous about something. "No. Not a lot. Plus I'd rather not say. If people find out what Thomas does with the beetles, Thomas could be in a lot of trouble…"

"Hey, it's okay Thomas, forget about it." 3Cube is feeling that pang of guilt again. "Look, I'll just grab the usual and then I'll get out of your way, okay?"

Thomas' mood lifts instantly. "Yes! Yes! The usual! The usual! Two colours!" In a flurry of activity the old man spins around and disappears into the nearest tent, before emerging with two dirty-looking plastic bottles, both splattered with black and white flecks. With black and white stained hands he excitedly attaches them to two tubes that emerge from around the back of the cages, before typing frantically on an impossibly old and filthy laptop balanced on a nearby stack of milk crates.

Without warning the contents of every cage stir into life, the suddenness enough to make 3Cube take two whole steps backwards. In front of him the hatches are full of life and movement, shuffling and twitching, and a cacophony of whirring and low beeps. Within seconds the two plastic bottles are being filled by the spurting of beetle juice, one filling with black and one with white. Two colours.

3Cube holds his ground, breathing hard to fight back the fear and the urge to run. He can't remember how long he's had this irrational phobia of the beetles, but it feels like it has always been with him. He knows they are just robots; dumb, harmless little cleaning machines, but there's something about them that's just not right. Maybe its knowing that they are full of millions and millions of those tiny little writhing invisible nano-machines, he thinks. But he handles beetle juice almost every day, and that doesn't scare him on its own, apart from occasionally freaking him out when he can smell the fumes and imagines them all climbing up his nose.

No, he knows what it is. It's the way they move. The way they can seem completely still one second, and then twitchy and alive the next. It's the way they seem like they are breathing and reacting even though they're just metal and plastic. It's the way their horrifically angled legs are dead and silent one moment, flexing and jerking the next. Thomas once told him that when they invented the first beetles they couldn't get them to move right, and in order to save money and time they scanned the brains of actual real living insects and installed them inside. 3Cube doesn't know if that's true, but it would explain a lot. And if anyone knows anything about beetles it's Thomas. No one knows more about them than him.

"Hey Thomas, do you think the beetles... do you think they feel anything?"

Thomas looks confused for a second or two, as if he doesn't understand what 3Cube is asking him. And then he just smiles, his eyes wide from either madness or beetle juice fumes.

"Two colours" he beams with autistic glee. "Two colours! Both black and white!"

*

3Cube's feet hurt. Constant drizzle. The thumbs-up from Tera's icon. Stencils. Beetle juice. Yet another Coca-Cola billboard.

This one is above one of the entrances to Cabot's Circus, a red and white banner heralding visitors to Bristol's central shopping district. It's almost twice as wide as the previous boards, and it's meant to be the epic finale of 3Cube's trilogy. It's also high up, and he nearly breaks his neck when his Nikes slip on damp steel as he clambers back down the fire escape.

Safely on the ground he gazes back up at his freshly juiced QR code and activates it. Instead of a hole being blown through the billboard, this time cracks start to spread across its glossy surface – slowly at first, and then increasingly quickly – until the whole thing falls to the ground. Shards shatter against concrete, unleashing a fine dust cloud that obscures his vision for a few seconds.

As quickly as the dust has risen it clears, and he's looking through the billboard at the Barton Hill towers again, this time from a completely different angle. But the cracking hasn't ended; fissures appear in the Bristol landscape and it's obvious that the city is being rocked by an earthquake, the towers themselves visibly shaking against the grey sky.

The cracking spreads from the ground to the towers themselves. As frothy seawater explodes from the fissures under the city the concrete facades fall from the towers, revealing unbreakable cliff faces studded with patches of vegetation, rising from the now-tranquil waters of the flooded city. Finally the grey sky above cracks, fragments of cloud falling and dissolving in the new urban ocean, as 3Cube is bathed in sunlight so warm-looking he can almost *feel* it.

3Cube has spent the last 24 hours wracked with doubt, but now that has gone. This is his final statement about how he feels his city – his home – can unleash its vibrancy through defiance of those that would attempt to control and regulate space. The city's space. His space.

An angry buzzing behind his ears, and Tera's icon gives him the thumbs-down.

Time to move.

3Cube freezes. He lets a few seconds of self-doubt pass, and then he removes his spex, killing the buzzing. He slips them into a padded pocket and flips his bag back onto his back. Next he's sprinting away from the billboard, across the few metres of pavement to the shops opposite. Then he's climbing, his fingers finding handholds in the ridges of a Tesco Metro's anti-riot shielding. He's not done this for years, not since the early days of his writing career - the days when being a writer involved almost as much parkour as it did knowing how to hold a spray can. It's exhilarating. He knows it's risky too - this being perhaps the most CCTV-saturated part of Bristol - but that just makes it all the more exciting. Plus he's quick. Within a few seconds he's on top of the roof, squatting between slowly-turning wind turbines, catching his breath.

He's now level with the billboard, separated from him by just a dozen or so metres of air. A perfect view. Nobody is going to get past him from here. All he has to do is wait, all night if necessary.

He sits down on the flat roof, his back against the gentle hum of an air conditioning unit. He zips up his stormsuit until only his eyes can be seen from under its fur-trimmed hood. Somewhere above him he can hear the faint drone of a passing police UAV; a single red light blinking in the dark sky.

*

Bristol was drowning. The drizzle had turned into torrential rain, alternating black and white droplets falling from the heavens. As they hit the forest of decaying architecture they splattered it with toxic paint; acid burning into concrete as clouds of suffocating fumes filled the war-torn streets. With an insidious clanking and scratching the beetles started to emerge from the gutters and alleys in their thousands, mouths turned up to the sky to drink in the poisonous rain...

*

3Cube is ripped from his nightmares by the insidious clanking and scratching.

He doesn't know how long he's been asleep. It's still dark, and even with his storm suit cranked up to max he can feel the cold night air. He pulls his hood back to let the air in, letting it refresh him. Hopefully he's not slept through anything important. He rubs his eyes and looks across to the billboard.

Its beetle has emerged, and with terrifyingly organic motion, is descending down the front of the billboard.

3Cube pushes himself to his feet, confused and startled. It isn't meant to be happening like this. He knows the beetles will come and destroy his work, they always do, but not yet. Not so quickly. Not before anyone has even seen it.

An initial flood of panic is drowned out by rage, and he wants to hurl something. He glances around the rooftop for potential missiles, but: nothing. He steps to the roof's edge and looks down and along the street, the initial rush of vertigo mixing with confusion - Cabot's Circus is empty. He expects to see the JCDecaux van and its funny little driver, but: nothing. Silence, except for the cooing of pigeons. Even the beetle is quiet now.

3Cube glances up. The beetle has stopped moving, even though it's a good six feet away from his QR Code. It's frozen in place, and 3Cube wonders if it is broken.

The silence is broken by more scratching and clanking.

Another beetle has emerged, this one from the other end of the larger-than-average billboard. A two-beetle board, thinks 3Cube. He's heard of them, but never seen one in action. But then he's never bombed anything this big before.

The second beetle descends until it is level with the first, which then stirs into life again, the two robots moving in unison. They scuttle left and right, crablike, moving in a flurry of multi-limbed horror, faster than 3Cube has seen them ever move before. And as they creep and crawl they keep their heads pointed towards the billboard's surface, spitting black and white beetle juice onto its glossy coating.

At first 3Cube still thinks they must be malfunctioning; performing some macabre, haywire dance. But as he watches very quickly the realisation hits him, so hard in fact that he feels his legs almost give way, and lowers himself back down onto the roof, his back once more against the AC unit.

The beetles are rendering an image, line by line, like the dual heads of a huge, ancient inkjet printer.

3Cube isn't sure how long he has been watching them by the time they've finished, but it is starting to get light. A couple of hours, minimum. What they have created is huge; a vast burn the width of the billboard. The towers of Barton Hill are disintegrating silhouettes against a blindingly white blast, a black mushroom cloud rising in the background, the city below them splitting into deep cracks and fissures. It is a far more simple image than the two previous works, and more starkly effective as a result. Something clicks in 3Cube's head as understanding takes control, and the beetles start their slow accent back to their nest.

*

The police are already wheeling Tera out of the entrance to the squats when 3Cube gets to the harbour side. He's ran most of the way there, and as he slows and catches his breath one of the cops spots him from behind his police issue Oakley spex. He steps forward and raises a hand to stop 3Cube.

"I need to talk to him. Please. Just a couple of minutes."

"He's under arrest. He's not going to be talking to anyone apart from us now, mate."

"Please" Tera says from behind the cop, his voice hollow from exhaustion and defeat. "Let me talk to him. I owe him an explanation".

The cop glances at Tera then back at 3Cube, and raises a single finger. "One minute".

3Cube pushes past him, and drops to one knee so he is level with the hacker.

"I'm sorry- " starts Tera.

"No man. No. Don't apologise. I understand now. I get it- "

"No man, you don't- "

"No! I do. I get it. I understand what you were trying to say, about how everything is so... fleeting. Trivial... too many colours, too much digital noise. And to make something permanent and handcrafted, but with machines- "

"No-"

"And so stark! So bold, man. Shit, you made my toys look like some played out shit. It's like- "

"'Cube! Shut up man. Really. You've got it wrong." Tera looks down at his useless legs, embarrassed. "It wasn't about any of that. It was just about the money."

Stunned silence.

"The money...? Who- "

"JCDecaux. It was a viral stunt man. They were worried about losing the Coke contract. Everyone's pulling out of billboards, the market is about to implode. Everybody just walks around with their spex on, looking at their own content. They just wanted a reason to make people look at the billboards, so they could get their blink-through numbers up."

3Cube is speechless.

"I'm sorry man. Part of the deal was that I painted over an established AR writer, so that they could build hype in the timelines. I'm sorry it had to be you, but that's the reason it was. It had to be someone with a rep."

"But... what? So what now?" 3Cube points at the cops, and their waiting van. "You just get locked up now?"

"Hopefully not. I should just get a fine. I've gotta keep quiet about JCDecaux, and in turn they're sorting me out with a lawyer. And then when it's all over I get paid. And I get my spine fixed, man. I get my legs back."

And as if on cue, two cops pick up Tera - wheelchair and all - and load him into the back of their van, and the last thing 3Cube sees of him is his damp eyes as they close the doors.

*

The contents of the Halfords bag make a clinking sound as 3Cube drops it on entering his room. Next he's ripping shit down from his wall; old QR Code stickers, pictures of Brazilian porn stars, the faded, tea-stained poster of Leo Kim. Within a few minutes he's cleared a section of wall three metres across, and as high as the ceiling. Bare wall, Bristol City Council regulation-issue magnolia paint.

He steps back, examines it.

Then he's moving again, his hand darting into the Halfords bag. It pulls out an aerosol can of car-repair spray, black. He sets it down on his desk, and pulls out a second, white. He rips off the lid, points the nozzle at the wall, and squeezes.

Paparazzi

When John got off the bus outside the Hippodrome Claire was nowhere to be seen. Instead she'd dropped a Post-it for him; a translucent slice of virtual A4 spinning slowly in the air at head height. He sighed and blinked at it, the note stopping its spin instantly to face him and just one word appearing on its surface: Starbucks. "Great" he muttered to himself, "but which fucking one?"

He blinked at the Google Earth logo on the note's bottom right corner and a football-sized coffee bean materialised in the air next to it, followed by another identical one three metres away, and then half a second later another, and then another and another; so that within a few seconds a trail of them hung in the air, disappearing into the crowd of afternoon shoppers and snaking up the hill along Park Street. High in the sunny Bristol sky he could see a ten metre high latte hanging like a hot-air balloon, the huge green arrow suspended from its underside pointing down at the store's location.

This was starting to turn into an Easter egg hunt. He'd never met Claire in the flesh before, but the contact he'd had with the girl so far had left him with little reason to suspect that this was some kind of griefer prank. He logged into WhereImAt, blinking through menus to pull up his Friends List, but she was still showing her location as private. Absentmindedly he scanned the other names on the list; Alice and Stefen were back at home, most of the day jobbers were at work, but Dave was in The White Bear just around the corner, having his customary afternoon pint.

John pushed his Samsung spex up onto his forehead, the menus and coffee beans vanishing from his view, and rubbed the bridge of his nose. The White Bear was a lot closer than the trek up Park Street, and right now beer seemed more appropriate than a caffeine hit. He hadn't been outside for maybe a week - he wasn't entirely sure - and the noise and chaos of Bristol city centre was making him tense and self-conscious. A dark, quiet pub would certainly be preferable, but one drink with Dave would lead to a second, and that was something his current financial status wouldn't really permit if he didn't want to live on microwaved dhal for the next fortnight. And even if Claire's promise of an actual paid job turned out to be bullshit, he was sure she'd mentioned that she would pay for the coffee. He slipped the spex back down over his eyes, and reluctantly started to follow the trail of beans.

*

"I'm sorry for all the messing around," Claire said, peering at him through her sleek Apple spex. "For all the... secret agent nonsense. But what I need to discuss with you is extremely sensitive. If it was to be heard by the wrong ears it could have grave ramifications not only for the two of us, but also for several of my Guild's top ranking officials."

John stifled a laugh, successfully managing to avoid snorting hot espresso down through his nose. It wasn't just the pomposity of how she talked about Guild business that amused him - he'd sadly become all too accustomed to how self-important gamers spoke about their characters and clans - it was more what she seemed to be suggesting.

"Sorry, you're telling me this Starbucks is more secure then us just discussing this in Third Person?"

"It is right now, yes." She sipped her latte. "I have friends making sure it is. But they couldn't give me a venue until the very last second, hence the running around. Again, I'm sorry, but I kind of had no choice."

Impressive, John thought, if true. Again he had all too much experience of clan kiddies unquestioningly spouting Guild doctrine, naively believing their leaders' claims to be real-life elite hackers, industry insiders, glamour models or re-turning messiahs. But Claire didn't really fit that stereotype; she was older for a start, and seemed more experienced, less gullible with it. Apart from the trendy Apple spex, the rest of her rig suggested functionality over style, her apparently hand knitted voice-free choker and fingerless data gloves in matching purple wool clearly old and starting to fray in places. He guessed she wore them partly out of comfort and famil-iarity and partly out of pride, the DIY aesthetic they implied considered to be a badge of status amongst members of her Crafter class. He imagined her sitting in her college room late into the night, knitting the gloves; carefully incorporating the Bluetooth transmitters, fibre optic sensors and RFID tags into their design. Jesus, the calibration alone must have taken her hours. As someone who had never used anything except In-dian- or Chinese-made off-the-shelf components, he had to admit he was impressed.

"Even though I've been assured this place is secure from external taps, I still don't want to risk us being overheard."

John glanced round the empty coffee shop. "It's dead. There's no one here."

"Still, we can't be too careful. You do have a choker on you, right?"

"Sure" John replied, reluctantly. He fished around in the side pocket of his cargo pants, and pulled out a cheap Logitech-branded voice-free choker. He always carried it on him, but hated wearing the bloody thing as it made the skin on his neck itch, especially on hot days like this one. He wrapped it tightly around his throat; fastening the two velcro ends together behind his neck. A small, red, ring-like icon appeared in the top corner of his field of view, quickly flicking to green as his spex established a connection with the choker and confirmed it was already eavesdropping on the weak electrical impulses being sent to his larynx.

A private space invitation from Claire instantly appeared in the air a foot in front of his face, and vanished just as quickly as he blinked his acceptance. Claire spoke again, without moving her lips, and her voice came not from her mouth but from behind his ears. The cheap noise-cancelling micro-speakers at the end of both of his spex's arms made her avatar-voice seem tinny, but at the same time cleaner, more confident; reminding John that he was listening to nothing more than Claire's spex running a virt-model of her larynx, probably built from a high street CAT scan, and undoubtedly tweaked with cosmetic software.

"You hear me?"

"Sure." he replied silently.

She cleared a space on the table between them, moving their drinks and discarded sweetener packets to one side, and then traced a lime green, dotted line on the flat surface with one finger. The line became a rectangle as her finger returned to its starting point, and became a two dimensional opaque slab floating a few millimetres off the table. Then suddenly it was a web browser window, filling with images of brightly coloured cartoon samurai and warrior monks, animations of stylistic monsters and burning villages, and what John guessed was Korean text. Game stuff. Claire reached over and lightly touched the largest image, a head-shot of a handsome but heavily-stylized Asian male, his long, dark hair pulled back in the traditional samurai style, his eyes narrowed into a cold, aggressive steely gaze. John couldn't work out if it was a heavily-tweaked photo, a render or a mixture of the two. Either way it looked slightly absurd to him, camp even. He wanted to laugh, but he resisted it again.

"You know who this is, right?" Claire said.

John shrugged. "No idea."

"Really?" she replied, the avatar-voice model doing the best it could to convey her disbelief. "Don't you ever watch the news? That's Leo Kim, one of the highest-ranking *A Wind of Blades* players this side of the Great Firewall. He was voted Sakura Guild's most valued player three years- "

"Look," John interrupted, still trying not to laugh. "Believe it or not, I don't know him. I don't play *Blades* and I don't really go in for celebrity watching."

"Fair enough" Claire sighed. "But if you take this job, you're gonna have to start doing both."

John felt his cheeks flush hot with embarrassment and then, just as quickly, anger. Partly towards Claire for wasting his time, but overwhelmingly towards himself for not seeing this coming.

He pushed one hand down firmly on the table as if to push himself up and leave, and whipped his spex off his head with the other. "I think there's been a misunderstanding, and we're both wasting our time. What ever it is you think I do, I'm not paparazzi- "

"No," Claire interrupted. "You're a machinima documentary director. Arguably one of the best. I know, I've experienced *Ghosts of Fallujah* three times. From all the main POVs. It's a masterpiece."

John realised for the first time that Claire's hand was on his – an attempt to calm him and stop him from leaving – and it was working. He hadn't had any physical contact that intimate, that simple, for a long time, and it was making the hairs on the back of his neck start to stand upright. Embarrassed, he tried to shake the sensation.

"Then if you've seen *Ghosts* you know my work goes way beyond door stepping celebrities."

"Oh, of course. And as beautifully caught and edited as Ghosts was, it's not actually those skills we're primarily interested in." She removed her hand from his, and pointed towards the spex hanging limply from his right hand. "Please, hear me out."

Reluctantly he relaxed, returning the spex to his face. Her avatar voice returned, now sounding clinical and cold, especially without the touch of her skin on his.

"How long did you spend in that game, John?"

"It wasn't a game." he corrected her, annoyed. "It was a US military construct; a training sim. Stolen and cracked by a group of teenage Syrian hackers. It had a level of gritty realism you won't even have got a hint of from watching *Ghosts*. All in all I spent about 18 months in there."

"18 months, while they constantly fought and re-fought the Second Battle of Fallujah, 22 years after it really ended, until they got the result they had always wanted. And they never suspected a thing."

"Sorry?"

"About you. They never suspected once you were an outsider, right? They always just assumed you were one of them."

"Well, not exactly. They never thought I was Syrian. But I did manage to convince them I was a disenfranchised Muslim teenager from Bradford, yeah. There were quite a few European kids in there. They never suspected anything beyond that. I'm not going to pretend it wasn't hard work though."

"Of course. But you did it." She paused to sip her latte. "Look John, I can get any one of a thousand *Blades* wannabees I know to do this run for me, get them tooled up with illegal recording and capture warez, get them to grab a couple of hours of Kim doing his thing in game. But they wouldn't last ten minutes in there without him or one of his lackeys spotting them for who they really are. They'd be too sloppy, not cover their tracks properly. Anyone that enters a game-instance with a player at his level is going to be scrutinised to fuck, their bio and social profiles are going to have to be tight. You've already proved you can do that. If you can get past a bunch of jittery Jihadists, then some Korean cyber-athletes are going to be a piece of cake."

The flattery was working. John knew it was a cheap tactic, and he was falling for it. To be honest, it had been nearly two years since he'd discussed Ghosts with anyone, and even longer since anyone had heaped praise on it.

"You never followed Ghosts up though?" she asked him. "Did you make much from it?"

He chuckled quietly. "Nah, not really. There was a bit of interest in the first few months, but no one would touch it. None of the big ad networks, not Google, not the big providers... no one. I ended up broke, basically." He stared down into his coffee mug. "Look, I know where you're going. Yes, I'm skint. Well spotted. So put me out of my misery, what exactly would I get out of this run?"

"My Guild, Sentra-li, is prepared to cover all your initial set-up expenses. On top of that, you get whatever you can sell the footage you capture for."

John paused to take in what she'd said, it didn't make sense. "Sorry have I missed something? I get all the money for the footage? Not just a percentage? I don't- "

"This isn't about financial gain John, at least not for my people. This is very, very personal."

She pointed down at the browser window suspended above the table, at the stylised image of Leo Kim's avatar. "This run isn't just an average dungeon-crawl. It's part of the beta test for Blades' new content release."

John stared back at her blankly. "And?"

She sighed. "*A Wind of Blades*.. .it's obsessed... its players, its Guilds, the game itself... they're all obsessed with status. Kim markets himself - his persona, everything - around an image of being an elite player, with ties to no one except his in-game Guild and his real-world sponsors. That's why my people became so interested when they found out he was working as a tester for the games dev team. The great Leo Kim running around still-unfinished code and filing bug reports? Apparently he still has some very firm ties with the developers. Imagine how damaging that would be for the brand he has built for himself if it got public."

John laughed. "So this... all this cloak and dagger stuff... it's just so you can embarrass someone?"

Claire fixed him with a stare that made it perfectly clear that she felt nothing of what she had said was in the slightest bit amusing. "Leo Kim isn't just a good Blades player, but one of their most revered generals. Mainly due to the profile he has built for himself. He could say the word and a thousand Sakura members would fall on their own swords. Last season, during an unscheduled and unprovoked land-grab, he successfully led eight hundred troops into Sentra-li territory and surrounded one of our outermost fortresses. The siege was ultimately successful, but not until three weeks had passed and hundreds of my people had to coldly stare perma-death in the face."

John again stifled a laugh at her pompous language. Of course he comprehended the emotional and financial attachment career gamers like Claire built up with well developed characters over years of investing in and role-playing them, but he always found the quasi-religious fixation with perma-death – the mortal wounding of an avatar in a way or location that didn't permit any resuscitation - somewhat laughable. Perhaps it was because he'd watched dozens of Muslim teenagers use their own beloved, lovingly self-crafted alter egos as sacrificial weapons, apparently without ever a second of hesitation; their own personal beliefs transcending concerns of finance or game ranking. It had certainly shifted his perspective on a few things.

"So this is mainly about revenge and political instability then? Nothing changes, I guess." He looked her firmly in the eyes. "So what if I was actually interested? What happens then?"

Claire smiled back it him, a hint of playful glee in her eye. " Then I'd suggest you get into training pretty quickly. The run is scheduled for just over two weeks' time. You're a *Blades* virgin. You've a lot to learn."

"But what about a character? Where the hell do I get one?"

"Oh, don't worry." She smiled wryly and sipped her latte again. "Leave that to us."

*

John opened the door to the kitchen to find the air thick with Post-its and the smell of over-processed food. His housemate Alice was responsible for the Post-its, the usual nagging reminders to the other occupants to wash up and buy milk, but it was Stefen, sitting at the kitchen table eating instant noodles and reading a copy of the Bristol Evening News, that was responsible for the unappetising aroma.

"Jesus, man," he said to Stefen, "who does she think she fucking is, our mum?"

Stefen looked up at him blankly. "Sorry?"

"Alice, man. The Post-its?"

"Ah. You see my friend, I never break my first rule."

"First rule?"

"Ja." He grinned and tapped the side his left eye socket with one finger. "Never wear your spex in the kitchen."

John laughed, but promptly removed his Samsungs and dumped them on the table as though it was the best advice he'd ever heard. John had a lot of time for Stefen; for a low-level career gamer he displayed a surprisingly dry sense of humour, and a healthy disregard for the usual social conventions of an undoubtedly Guild-dominated life. But in truth John realised that he didn't really know or connect with the young Hungarian as much as he might wish. It was the same with the other four occupants of the small Bedminster terraced house with whom he shared the rent, and he'd resigned himself to the fact that it would probably always be that way. It was the inevitable consequence of living solely with people who had decided to dedicate their lives and careers to the virtual. They were companions only due to some seemingly outmoded geographical and economic meatspace necessity, and they all understood it, ever aware that however close they may become to one another, all their true friendships and allegiances lay elsewhere.

Except maybe for John, who was without those kinds of friends or allies; the people he once put in those categories had turned their backs on him amid rumours of fraud and betrayal, and abandoned their identities and fled into the deeper, darker parts of the net and away from those that would label them dissidents and terrorists.

"You seen this?" Stefen asked through a mouthful of piss-yellow noodles. "Chinese goldfarms. Says here that some of the Guilds are rounding up orphans from the floods and making them work twelve-hour shifts running game accounts. You know, making in game items and shit."

"So? What's new? Been going on for decades."

"Yeah, but these are kids man. Seven years old, it says here."

"Shit Stefen, you know better than believe what you read. Especially when its about China. All the western Guilds have got huge shares in the main media providers these days."

"Ja, ja, I know." he swallowed another mouthful of noodles. "But this… I dunno, I wouldn't be surprised man. These big Asian Guilds, y'know? They'll do anything for the edge. Anything."

John grabbed a glass of water and sat opposite Stefen at the table. "You know much about them?"

"Hey," Stefan smirked, "I read the papers."

"Sakura and Sentra-li, you know them?"

"Hell yeah, two of the biggies, across several titles, *A Wind of Blades* and *The Blood of our Heirs* mainly. Really nasty long-term rivalry between the two. Lots of big-ego, big-bucks star players on both sides. Lots of pride and bullshit. Endless power-struggles and soap opera tabloid drama at all levels. Why you asking?"

"Oh, nothing really." John replied. "Just some old college mates, trying to get me to sign up to one or the other. Can't even remember which."

Stefen snorted. "Well my friend, one piece of advice to you before you make a decision like that: Google hard. Make sure you know what you're getting into, and that these old friends are good friends. I'd keep looking over my shoulder if I was involved with either of those organisations, man, and God forgive anyone that finds themselves caught between the two."

*

Up in his room, John booted his Toshiba desktop and removed the Sony headset from its recharging cradle. He sat in the tattered Ikea office chair and slipped the skeletal, lightweight headset on, fitting it snugly round his skull with what felt like cold, bony, plastic fingers. He adjusted the goggles so they completely sealed his eye sockets and no external light could permeate, the total darkness lasting only momentarily before the lasers started to project images directly onto his retinas.

His computer's desktop unravelled into existence around him, an ornately tiled recreation of his favourite Fallujah roof garden, the city's familiar yet still magnificent minarets dominating the skyline. It was the perfect facsimile of the roof of a real building that hadn't existed for over two decades; reduced to rubble and dust by air strikes and artillery fire.

John focused on a mental short cut, and a browser window appeared floating in the air in front of his face, the sensors in the headset's fingers detecting the faint signal of his brain waves. The hardware manufacturers liked to call it a "Brain Computer Interface", which always made John smile. It was infinitely less sophisticated than the marketing suggested; the system worked by showing the user simple icons while looking for subtle, corresponding changes in the brain's magnetic field. The user then had to memorise the icons, and recall them to prompt the computer into acting. It was pretty unsophisticated - firmly one way, hit and miss at times, and necessitated a lot of practice on the users part initially - but it was a popular system. In fact, in some ways it was the system's shortcomings that had made it the most widely adopted input method with gamers; the need to put time and effort in giving it a slightly macho edge. Being good at 'focussing' was a sought-after and valuable skill that brought both financial rewards and status, and was often discussed in near mystical terms by disturbingly large swathes of the gaming community.

He navigated the browser to the *A Wind of Blades* website, and promptly started to download the free client software, which slowly materialised on the roof garden's floor as a dully glowing cube. It was a big file and was going to take a while, so he opened his mail client. Amongst the junk and spam there was already an email from Claire - she was evidently a fast worker. He opened the heavily encrypted message and scanned its contents. There were sign-in details for a *Blades* account, which Sentra-li had set up for him, and an unnamed attachment. He unpacked it onto the roof garden, but it appeared as a nondescript black cube; useless data until the *Blades* client was installed. All he could assume, from the levels of encryption that Claire had used, was that it was of a sensitive and possibly legally-dubious nature.

He pulled the headset off and slumped back in the chair, rubbing his temples. What the hell was he getting himself into? This wasn't him, his world. This wasn't what he did. He avoided this sort of shit these days. His own first rule. But something had touched him about Claire - she'd known which buttons to press. She, or her people, had undoubtedly spent plenty of time researching him, his bios, his social networking profiles, until they knew exactly which angle to take to get him on board. And even though part of him felt like a fool for falling so easily for it, he couldn't deny that he was relishing the challenge.

Plus, he really did need the money.

The Toshiba chimed to notify him that the Blades download had completed. He sighed, and with a certain degree of trepidation, put the headset back on.

On the rooftop, the Blades client was already unpacking and installing itself. The cube unfolded itself into six separate windows, three of which were showing the usual high-budget but bland and predictable opening movies, while two showed similarly predictable terms and conditions, legal disclaimers and end-user licence agreements. It was the last one that caught his attention; the log-in/registration screen. With a mixture of focusing and hand gestures he cut and pasted the relevant information from Claire's email into the form.

A Wind of Blades unwrapped itself around him. He was stood on top of a valley, the sides of which had been cut into large flat steps, each of which held paddy fields with tiny-looking figures toiling away in between the rice plants. Directly below him at the bottom of the valley, led to by a long winding path, was a large walled city, topped by towering pagodas, watchtowers, and hundreds of brightly coloured flags. The entire scene had an unreal quality, looking as though it had almost been hand painted, and despite its generic anime style, John had to admit the sheer scale of it all impressed him.

He looked down at his hands, the Toshiba watching his head and body movements and syncing his avatar perfectly. Ornate rings, engraved with unknown Asian characters and studded with small jewels, graced most of his fingers. He focused and zoomed out to third person, the usual, wrenching feeling of disembodiment grasping him at first, and slowly rotated around the character.

"Well, at least he's male." was his first reaction. The character was minimally dressed, in the traditional Ronin style, with just a simple purple kimono as the main garment, but with a never-ending selection of items and weapons hanging from straps and belts. Despite giving an initial impression of scruffiness, the character oozed status and experience. Perfect, he thought. It was emphasised even more when he rotated round so that he was looking the avatar directly in the face. The character was Asian, in what appeared to be his mid-thirties, and handsome save for two parallel sword scars that ran down the right side of his face from the eye socket to the bottom of the cheek. Without warning the face grinned back at him, making him jump, until he realised it was only mimicking his own facial expression. Maybe this was all going to be more fun then he had first imagined.

He jumped back into first person, and tried a standard focus command for opening in-game menus. The air around his face erupted with windows, overloading him with information - inventory lists, statistics, skills, wound status reports, chi levels, friend lists. Almost as quickly as they appeared, he focused again and shut them all down. Too much. Claire was right, he thought, he had a lot to learn.

Silently he started the walk down the long road to the city below.

*

John rubbed his tired eyes and squinted at the Toshiba's LCD display, trying to read the game log. Over the last two weeks he had apparently spent 156.34 hours in-game, running through tutorials and quests, getting a feel for not only his character and the controls, but also the game world itself. It was a sizable chunk of his life, but he couldn't shake the feeling that it wasn't enough. The character Claire had supplied him with was developed and powerful, more than capable of handling anything that might be thrown at him during the simple beta-test run, but only as long as he could control it. And, more importantly, make it look convincing.

It wasn't all he'd been doing over the last fortnight. He had spent almost as much time elsewhere in the net, flitting between forums and social networking sites, building up his fake identity. It was a long and complicated process, constructing a believable alter ego, laying a digital trail around the net that gave the impression that a real person had passed through, but he was one of the best he knew at it. Months of constantly shifting and updating his trail while working on *Ghosts* had made him an expert, and in many ways he found it more challenging and enjoyable than playing the game itself. But even now he wasn't convinced that he had enough to keep the Sakura Guild spies off his back.

There wasn't time to worry about it now. He lay back on his bed and set his alarm clock for 5am. Just three short hours, and the run would be under way.

*

Claire laughed, in that way she always did, with her head tilted back and her eyes closed. It wasn't the first time he'd seen her in-game - they'd done half a dozen or more practice runs together over the last couple of weeks - but something about the elegance of her avatar always caught his breath; the dark strands of her cell-shaded hair moving in the gentle breeze. When he first met her she had seemed somewhat self-important and humourless to John, but over the last two weeks his perception had changed. They had fun together, despite the heavy training regime she had been running him through, and he seemed to be able to make her laugh. And when she did it made something inside him flutter, and the hairs on the back of his neck twitch. He'd had to learn to mute some his avatar's emotional tracking, to hide the blushing.

"So how have you been finding it?" Claire asked. "Don't tell me you've been actually enjoying yourself?"

He paused at first, unsure what to say, a mixture of emotions hidden from her view as he temporarily disabled the avatar's ability to convey more than basic facial expressions. The last two weeks had been hard, stressful work, but with hindsight he wouldn't have missed it for the world. To his own surprise he had gradually felt his own bitter cynicism chipped away, replaced slowly with feelings of excitement and companionship and a sense of purpose he hadn't experienced since Fallujah. He wanted to tell Claire, more than anyone, all of this, to share his new enthusiasm with her, but looking at her now he just felt as awkward as always, and knew he wouldn't be able to find the words.

"You got me," he replied instead. "I haven't had so much fun in years. And this spot... the view here always impresses me."

They were stood on the same spot where he had first entered the game, overlooking the rice plantations and the city below. "It's the attention to detail." he continued, "I mean, those bots tending to the paddy fields, they move so realistically. I've watched them, and they never seem to repeat what they do. It's almost as though they're not just animation loops."

"They're not bots, John."

"Huh?"

"They're real players. Sentra-li Guild members."

"What?" They... they log in here just to do that? To pick rice?"

"It's an honourable profession. A vital one. Those rice balls you eat when your health and chi is low? They're all made in places like this. It's *Blades'* most important currency, John. An army marches on its stomach."

"But... but why? Why come here, with all this place has to offer, and do that? By choice?"

"They have their reasons." Claire said, guardedly. "Money. Guild progression. Honour. It's not that unusual, really. But come, let's get a move on. We don't want to keep the others waiting."

Together they started the long walk down the hill.

*

When they entered the beta-instant, three figures were already waiting for them in a clearing in the woods. They all wore the familiar Sakura Guild attire, but it was obvious at first glance which one was Leo Kim. He towered above the other players, not purely in stature, but more in presence. There was something about the way he carried himself, his self-confidence, which John couldn't quite put his finger on. Sure his costume was slightly more elaborate, he had more trinkets and ornately crafted weapons hanging from his belt, but there was something else. It was something he'd only experienced once or twice before, in either the real or the virtual. But it was unmistakable.

And then, as Leo Kim calmly introduced himself, he realised what it was. It was celebrity.

Kim spoke little, exchanging little more than pleasantries with Claire, the tension of generations-old inter-Guild rivalry hanging heavy in the air between them at all times. Under any other circumstances they would never have been in such close proximity, save for a chance encounter on a battlefield, but it was apparently part of the developer's beta regulations that no new quest content be tested by single Guild parties.

Pleasantries aside, the quest began. The clearing around them seemed to spin and distort as the game transferred them to the new quest area. The transition effect always made John feel nauseous, and instinctively he shut his eyes. On opening them again he had to catch his breath. Claire had explained to him that they were going to be testing a major content upgrade;

something new and fresh to ensure that the more casual players and Guild members retained their interest and kept paying their subs, and now John could see exactly what she meant. In the mere couple of weeks that he'd been playing, he'd not yet seen an environment quite like this.

They were stood on the edge of a low cliff, looking down across what appeared to the ruins of an ancient, abandoned city; parts of which were flooded by silver pools of water, while others were almost entirely obscured by overgrown jungle. It was the architecture that seemed so unusual, a strange mix of Mayan and Edo-era Japanese, giant statues of kings and warriors with anime features emerging defiantly from the floodwaters and impossibly tall pagodas entwined in vines. Everything seemed to be carved from the same somewhat alien looking jade-coloured stone, but as fantastical as it all seemed John again couldn't help but be convinced by the sheer scale.

There was a rustle in the undergrowth to their left, and a short fat man - clearly a pre-scripted bot - emerged from the bushes. He stood in front of the party, breathing painfully with blood pouring from a gaping wound in his side, soaking the rag-like farmers' clothes he wore. The bot began to babble something in a language John didn't understand, either Japanese or Korean.

He quickly shot Claire a private message. 'I can't understand what he's fucking saying.'

'Cos they haven't localised it yet.' she replied. 'Just chill.'

"It's the usual bullshit." one of the Sakura players said, with unnerving timing. "He's part of an archaeological expedition that has been attacked by Tanuki. We need to fight through and rescue everyone, and retrieve some artefact they've uncovered."

"What the hell are Tanuki?" the other Sakura player asked.

"They're a kind of Yokai" Claire replied. "Japanese folklore creatures. Kind of part human, part raccoon. Live in the woods and play shape-shifting tricks on travellers. Though looking at that bot's wounds I'm guessing they're not interested in just conning us out of some sake."

The fat little archaeologist had collapsed at their feet, gurgling in a pool of his own blood.

"They're near" said Leo Kim, calmly.

As if on his cue, dozens of shifting, black hooded figures erupted from between the trees clasping crude-looking weapons and emitting low, animal-like growls. Instinctively John jumped into third person and started to focus on his attack combinations, watching his avatar swirling into the ranks of Tanuki, Katana swords outstretched. It was no longer responding to his real body's movements, instead relying on his ability to remember the ever increasingly elaborate strings of focus moves, as the air filled with the Tanuki's dark blood and pained screams. As he sliced through one of the disgusting creatures' twisted snouts, he glanced around to see the other players disappearing into their own chaotic, violent blurs. He caught Leo Kim parrying a Tanuki Shaman's lightning blasts with a Katana sword in his left hand, whilst removing the arm from a foot soldier with a second blade in his right, the creature exhaling wetly as its corpse went limp and fell to the floor in a mist of black blood. John found himself gazing at Kim in awe at how elegantly and effortlessly he twirled through his attack and defence combos, part theatrical martial artist, part ballet dancer, before he suddenly remembered what he was actually here to do.

Popping out of the *Blades* client for a moment, he quickly activated the attachment Claire had sent him two weeks previously. It instantly unpacked itself, without any flurry or flash, and presented one simple message window:

FORCED CAPTURE ENABLED - RECORDING

It was a *Blades* recording script. Like most of the popular titles, *Blades* didn't permit the recording of in-game events without all participants' prior consent. It was a measure to protect individual privacy, and to stop paparazzi like John from doing exactly what he was doing right now. With the script running, he jumped back into the game.

To find the violence over, and the other players staring at him.

"What's wrong, comrade?" asked one of the Sakura warriors. "You froze up."

"Apologies," John replied. "I had some really bad lag, almost thought I'd have to log out. What happened here?"

"We killed them all" said Claire. "We need to move to the next area. Can you carry on?"

"Oh, sure. It was weird though. Must be something in the beta code."

Leo Kim fixed him with a dominating stare. "Make sure that you report it to the devs when we are done."

And then he silently turned and strode down some beaten steps that descended into the vast city, the other players following him.

*

The run was over in less than two hours.

As he stood in the cold, stone hall of an abandoned temple, Tanuki bodies littered around his feet, John felt elated; more exhilarated than he had felt in years. But soon he found he had no one to share it with, as the other players grunted farewells and logged out of the game, vanishing before his eyes. Even Claire was gone before he could speak to her. No problem, he'd message her tomorrow. They could meet up maybe, celebrate. Go for a coffee again.

He logged out himself, and pulled off his headset, massaging his temples with the palms of his hands. He was torn, half of him wanting to play again, the other half craving sleep. But he knew neither was an option. He had footage to edit and sell.

*

John awoke on his bed, his head thumping, to the sound of rolling news. It was 10 am, and Leo Kim was stepping off a helicopter at a Florida flood relief camp, passing out plastic Katana swords to the refugee children that swarmed from the rows of identical FEMA caravans. The real-life, flesh and blood Leo Kim. It was the first time John had seen actual video footage of the player, but he knew it was him. He was a noticeably shorter, slightly imperfect facsimile of his avatar, right down to his outfit. Kim wore a real-life copy of his character's trademarked red kimono, complete with elaborate Guild embroidery. But in the harsh reality of the gray Florida light he looked more like an embarrassed cos-player then an anime superhero; the kimono seeming garish and flapping awkwardly in the gusting pre-hurricane winds rather than undulating elegantly in the gentle, non-existent, in-game breeze. The contrast was so stark at first that it actually made John laugh, until he squinted at the TV, and noticed the date stamp on the news footage said that it had been filmed five hours ago. When the run was still on.

Impossible. Even a player like Kim couldn't play and make a personal appearance at the same time. It made no sense at all. John's head was still full of edits, Tanuki and swordplay.

Unless it hadn't really been him on the run.

John panicked and gestured at the Toshiba to pull up the private auction he'd set up online. He'd slept through it all, but apparently hadn't really missed much at. The footage had sold, but for a fraction of what he had expected, its value discredited when the world had realised it must be fake.

John stood, struggling to find his balance after hours of moving only in the virtual, and stumbled around his room trying to find his spex so he could call Claire. He didn't get far though, before a Tanuki shaman burst through his bedroom door and fired a blue lightning bolt hard into his chest.

*

"Please, Mr Smith, don't get up," said a thick cockney accent, before he felt a hand on his chest, gently pushing him back down on to the bed.

A large, bulky figure sat above him, wearing a black double-breasted suit and Oakley military-issue spex. John's chest hurt, his limbs felt cold and sweaty, hot but noticeably shivering. "What... what did you do to me?"

"Oh, Mr Smith, it was just a little bit of taser." The man grinned coldly, his eyes still hidden behind the dark spex. "Don't tell me you've never been tasered before? I find that hard to believe, with your politically-dubious background."

"Who sent you?" John managed, struggling for breath. "Sakura?"

"Ahh, close, but not quite. I represent Sentra-li, believe it or not. It's my job to tie up loose ends."

"I don't understand... "

"Ah, my apologies. Let me show you. Careful now. Your body will still be quite weak." John reluctantly accepted the suited man's hand, as he helped him sit upright on the bed. His back ached, his head felt heavy, his arms numb. John had never had a heart attack, but this was how he guessed it must feel afterwards.

The man perched himself on the edge of the bed and gestured at the Toshiba, flicking it onto the Game Pipe News TV channel. Immediately he spoke, his voice full of sarcastic glee and patronising, mock surprise.

"Look, Mr Smith, the little film you made for us. It's on television. Well done!"

John squinted at the TV. It certainly did seem to be his footage, but there was something drastically different about it. There was no Leo Kim. In fact, there were no players at all. Someone had edited the captured data and removed them completely, leaving only footage of the new game environment. In fact they'd thrown out all of John's edits, trashing hours of work, and just used the raw positional data he'd recorded to create a selection of fly-throughs of the new lost city levels. John didn't get it at first. Then a headline appeared at the bottom of the screen that explained it all.

NEW BLADES BETA CONTENT - FOOTAGE LEAKED

"Let me give you a little background." the suited man said, jarring John's concentration. "I don't know whether you will have read about it, but about four weeks ago Sentra-li bought a thirty three percent stake in Game Pipe News Ltd. A big deal, and one that took a lot of negotiation. One of the things that finalised it was a promise by Sentra-li that it would use its considerable influence to provide GPN with a huge scoop on a major title. Just by luck, around that time Sentra managed to secure a limited number of places on a *Blades* beta test."

"But... Leo Kim... "

"I'm sorry Mr Smith, we were a little dishonest to you about Leo Kim. That wasn't him in game with you. It was an impostor. But we had to give you a reason, and the real one wouldn't have really done. You see, beta tests like the one you were involved in last night are highly confidential. Anyone that enters them - Guilds included - is subject to extremely tight Non Disclosure Agreements. In fact, as I speak right now, a team of lawyers is raiding the GPN offices in LA. And if they connect that footage to you, and in turn you to Sentra-li... well. I'm sure you can imagine the inconvenience that would cause to many people."

He leaned close, so that John could see his own terrified eyes reflected in the man's spex. "And that's why I'm here. Like I said. To clear up any loose ends."

John's mouth was dry. His muscles started to shake again, but not from the after affects of the taser this time.

"Look... please. Just... don't kill me... "

The man laughed. "Kill you? Oh no Mr Smith. We're not the Triads or the Mafia. We're not monsters. Plus anyway, death is such a terrible waste. Oh no, I have a vastly more profitable solution. Tell me Mr Smith, have you ever been to China?"

*

John found that if he imagined hard enough, he could almost smell the pollen and cherry blossom blowing up from the valley, instead of the smell of sweat, processed noodles and stale smoke that permeated into his consciousness from the real world.

As soul-destroying as constantly focussing on rice picking was, he still preferred being here to the depressing gloom of the sweatshop dormitory – crammed with a strange combination of desperate, poverty stricken farmers forced off their land by the ever advancing floods and over-privileged western students spending a gap year trying to impress the Guild - that smothered him whenever he removed his headset. When he could, he would take a few seconds' break to gaze at the view that had always fascinated and enthralled him. He liked it best as his shift approached its end, with the sun setting slowly on the horizon, turning the bird-filled sky pink and silhouetting the distant city's towers and pagodas. He would stare at them and dream of strolling down there one more time, his head held high again, until one of the gang masters spotted him slacking off, as they always did, and zapped him with an instant Work Credit Penalty. Or, even worse, threatened to revoke his daylight pass.

He had lost track of the weeks, but he knew he wouldn't be here forever. What he was doing here was honourable work; it wouldn't go unnoticed by the Guild. An army marches on its stomach. With time, they would recognise his loyalty and commitment, and they would let him leave here, sending him out into the world with just a sword and his honour, to make his mark among the great heroes.

Havana Augmented

When Paul ported into the Sakura compound, he found himself surrounded by crowds. He wasn't used to accessing public Third Person servers, especially ones as highly populated as this, and the number of bodies circulating around him was disorientating.

After a moment the panic subsided, and he found himself instead marvelling at the crowds of fans gathering around the walls of Kim's palace. Most of them wore some sort of cosplay avatar, or Sakura clan uniforms and *A Wind of Blades* kimonos. He smiled to himself when he spotted a small group near one of the translucent statues dressed in *Rolling Iron* pilot fatigues. He contemplated drifting over to talk to them, but wasn't sure what he would say. Looking around at the fans - all here desperate to catch a glimpse of their favourite game-idol in the non-flesh - none of them would believe him if he told them why he had come, decrying him as a yet another disillusioned guild fanatic.

He didn't need to wait long before the expected private space request opened in the air in front of his face, and the crowd faded into oblivion as he blinked his acceptance. For a few seconds he stood alone in the vast space around the fortress-like walls, the only sound the gentle flapping of the Sakura flags in the artificial breeze. Then the theatrics began.

A section of the wall folded down, drawbridge-style, and from within the dark halls a lone figure rode out towards him on a white, muscular, armour-clad unicorn. Paul found himself trying not to laugh; the pomposity of game-idols never failed to amuse him, but he stifled his true thoughts.

Kim leapt from his trophy mount in a flurry of pre-mocapped – and undoubtedly edited – elegance, and strode towards him. He looked, to Paul, just like the images he'd seen in Marcus' illegally-imported games magazines, or at least his avatar did: a slightly over-polished, almost awkward fusion of scruffy chanbara chic and red-carpet designer arrogance. To Paul's barrio eyes Kim seemed an almost absurd figure, but to the now-invisible throngs of adoring subjects, and to most people off-island Paul assumed, he symbolised the pinnacle of celebrity success.

They exchanged the traditional contact-free virt fist-bump, Kim welcoming him to his compound with a strange mix of superiority and what did seem to be genuine interest. Damn right, thought Paul, you should be interested. We've already made you even fucking richer.

"It's a pleasure to finally meet you Paul. I don't know how much you realise, but you're quite a celebrity in the gaming community outside of Cuba."

"I'd heard rumours" Paul replied, "but these things are often exaggerated."

Kim smiled. "Well, my hope is that if this all goes well your government will be persuaded to open up net access to all, and you and the rest of your lance will be able to bask in the glory you've so rightfully earned. It would be to the advantage of all, I think it's fair to say."

Advantage of all. For not the first time since he had been fronting these dealings with Sakura, Paul sensed that some wider motives were at play.

"Setting up this exhibition match has been a lot of work for us" Kim continued. "There has been a lot of, how can I put it, red tape involved."

"And a few bribes too, I'd guess." Paul added.

Kim laughed. "Yes, you're not wrong there. But we all – Sakura, Mindfield, our investors – we all feel it's a vital move. It would be easy for us to take what you and your friends have created in *Street Iron* and run with it, but we – and myself personally - think it's important that credit is given where it's due, and the world is given a chance to see how talented you all are."

Paul smirked inwardly. Translated: we could have taken your custom code and run because Cuban patent law is fucking non-existent; but the countless commentators, bloggers and Sakura-haters would never have let us live it down.

"Well, it's important to us and to the people of Havana. You can rest assured that my lance will play our best, especially with the will of Cuba behind us."

"I know you will." Kim smiled again, and gestured towards the open gate. "But come, we have much to discuss. And I should give you the tour. I'm sure you must be eager to see inside."

*

An hour had passed when Paul ported out, removing the heavy Venezuelan military-grade virt headset from his face. It was an archaic bit of kit, bulkier and less sophisticated than the illegally-imported Japanese sets that he and Marcus used. He gently rubbed his temples and the bridge of his nose as his eyes re-adjusted to actual light. Slowly the government office came into depressing focus.

The walls were standard-issue gray, blank except for the obligatory three faded portraits: Fidel, Raoul and of course Che. His two CDR handlers were there – he had forgotten their names weeks ago, referring to them simply as Good Cop and Bad Cop. Bad Cop leaned against the far wall, in between the two Castro brothers, a familiar sneer of bored contempt on his face. Good Cop sat at the opposite end of the interrogation table to Paul, puffing on one of his ever-present cigars, and smiled as he came into focus.

"So. How was our friend Mr Kim?" he asked.

"Well. We sorted out some of the finer details for the match. Some ground rules. Everything should be okay for next week."

"Excellent." Good Cop nodded and leant back in his seat, taking a long drag on his cigar before he spoke again. "Paul, I don't pretend to fully understand what it is that you and your friends have created, but the outside world seems to desire it, to place great value upon it. As such, it also of great value to Cuba."

Paul forced a gentle smile. He'd heard this lecture many times before.

"As I'm sure you know, our country has many times faced grave economic crisis. The last time was nearly thirty years ago, when our weaker comrades in the Soviet Union changed direction and abandoned us. Then, it was the strength and ingenuity of the Cuban people that pulled us through, as we made the transition to a tourist-based economy. But now that is under threat: the borders with America still to be fully opened; and the fuel crisis, and global warming meaning our European friends can no longer afford to visit here as they once did. As such, it is time for us to change again.

"Our new leader believes a free market is the way forward, and a digital one at that. We cannot do it alone, but our comrades in Central America have been lost in upheaval and change. This Sakura, though, they have exactly what we need. Along with the technology, they bring Chinese and Korean investment. It is imperative, while you show this Kim how adept Cubans are – how strong and fit for the fight – that you do not upset him, that he is not sent away with his tail between his legs, humiliated. Is that clear, comrade?"

"Of course" Paul replied. "The future of Cuba is always foremost in my thoughts."

"Excellent" Good Cop replied, a self-satisfied grin spreading across his face. "Now. Let us celebrate, hmm? Some rum perhaps? A good cigar?"

"Thank you comrade, but really – if it is possible - I would like to get home. I must see my family, and discuss today's events with the rest of my team, if that is acceptable?"

"Of course, of course! How rude of me, we will keep you no longer." He rose from his seat, gesturing towards Bad Cop. "Josef here will drive you back now."

The drive back to downtown Havana took a little under thirty minutes in the ageing but converted Lada. The noisy air conditioning pumped the fumes from the cooking fat-powered engine into the car, filling it with the smell of fried chicken. As always Bad Cop was surly and silent for the entire journey, so it surprised Paul that as they pulled up in front of the tenement where his family lived, he turned back to face him and spoke.

"Kim's palace" he said quietly. "He actually took you inside?"

"Si" Paul replied.

"And? What did it look like in there?"

"Gaudy" Paul responded, climbing out.

*

The next day, Paul went to meet Marcus in Parque Central. He found him sitting cross-legged under a palm, staring intently up into blank space, as though sun worshipping but in the wrong direction: his eyes shielded by his tinted spex. He seemed utterly focussed in deep meditation, until he caught Paul approaching in the periphery of his vision and his face cracked into a wide grin.

"Hola man." he said. "How was the big meeting with your

new showbiz buddy?"

"Like you'd expect." Paul replied. "He's a dick. More importantly, how are you getting on?"

"Good, man, good. Take a look." Marcus said, fishing a second pair of spex out of his kit bag and handing them to Paul, who promptly slipped them onto his face.

Instantly, Alphonso appeared, towering above them in the hot Havana air.

The seven metre high humanoid mech still maintained the majority of its original sleek, elegant Japanese *Hellcat* design, despite the heavy modifications Marcus had made to its frame over the last few years. The biggest change in the mech's appearance was the colouring; it boasted an over-waxed, gleaming green and white paint job that mimicked the famous retro-sheens Cuba's petrol-heads proudly gave to their seventy year old US muscle cars. In a similar way to how their love and care in maintaining their antique rides was a both a nod towards and a snub of their US designers in the face of decades of trade embargo; the finish that Marcus had given Alphonso was aimed squarely at the Japanese artist that had come up with the original *Hellcat* design. It sort of said 'Yeah. We like your work, but look what we've done with it now'.

Translucent windows hung in the air around Alphonso's towering frame, linked to various parts of his heavily-armoured body, each displaying differing statistics and data; ammunition levels, servo status, temperature readings. Glancing over the figures it was clear to Paul that Marcus had clearly made some important performance boosts already.

Paul smiled. Looking at Alphonso always made him smile. Mainly because Alphonso looked fucking bad-ass.

"I've tweaked the servos and the leg hydraulics code" Marcus explained, "which hopefully will sort out that suspension issue you were bitching about. And I've overhauled the coolant system on the chain gun to give you a little longer burst of time before it overheats. It's only a second or two, but, y'know. Could make a difference. The biggest change, though, is I completely reinstalled the targeting system's BIOS with a version I hacked a bit myself. Now it's strictly only beta at this point I guess, but in theory it should resolve that lag issue. In theory. If it don't work, or it makes it worse, I can always stick the original back on there."

Paul glanced over at Marcus with deep admiration. They had been close friends since Junior High, and for as long as he could remember Marcus had been obsessed with video games. It was an insanely hard hobby to follow in Cuba – the never-ending sanctions, the weak economy and the ever-limited net access making it almost impossible to get hold of anything game-related. But somehow Marcus had always found a way. Smugglers could be paid to bring in hardware, and legitimate net connections hijacked to grab pirated software. He always had to have the edge. Virt headsets and spex were rare – and technically illegal - on the island, with only a few hundred users that Paul knew of in Havana, but Marcus had been the first to own both.

The irony was that all through their years growing up together, Paul had always been the better gamer of the two; his reactions tighter, his focus more honed. Not that it bothered Marcus in the slightest. His interest in games wasn't about the competition, the bragging rights or the smack-talk. It was about the games themselves, the design, the code that made them work. Again, for as long as Paul could remember, Marcus had always tinkered and hacked away at any hardware or software he could get his hands on; making the games harder or easier, finding ways to cheat, finding – somehow – the online source code so that he could customise them. And not just games. When the hardware manufacturers and network providers wanted to augment-up Cuba and the paranoid government said no, together with a small group of fellow hackers he even set up Havana's first Spex AR space, from some thrown-together Google Earth data and strategically hidden, citywide, pirate radio style WIMAX routers. It would have been enough to have put him in a re-education centre for two years had he been caught, but the only people who ever knew about it loved Marcus – and the way he managed to feed their tech-lust cravings – too much to ever breathe a word.

With the flow of games into Cuba never more than a trickle, he kept the tiny little local gamer community alive with his own homebrew content, constantly expanding the lifespans of the few titles it could get its hands on. His love of games even got him a place at Havana University after they graduated high school – the only kid from their barrio that made it there – but Marcus dropped out after two semesters, frustrated by the tools he was given to play with, the retarded syllabus and the fact that his tutors seemed to be light years behind him in terms of comprehension. His decade-old dream of getting off-island and becoming a designer for one of the majors seemed destined to never materialise.

That was, until the whole *Rolling Iron thing* happened.

Rolling Iron was a Japanese mecha combat virt-game, developed by Kyoto dev team Mindfield and published by Sony. Players commanded large military robots through virtual arenas, fighting one-on-one or in teams of three known as Lances. Its only unique selling point at the time was that it was the first competitive mecha game to rely completely on focus-control. Most similar titles at the time used some kind of physical control pad or gesture-based input, but *RI* rejected all that, forcing the player to control the mechs through the simple brainwave-reading interface that had become standard on virt headsets at that point. While the system was common on role-playing games and strategy titles, it had until this point been considered too slow and inaccurate for fast-moving shooters. But someone in Kyoto had pulled out all the stops on both code and interface design, and proved it could work.

Even with this ace up its sleeve, *Rolling Iron* entered a crowded market for mech-shooters, and probably would have disappeared largely without trace if it hadn't have been for Sony somehow convincing a couple of the largest gaming guilds - the true wielders of influence in the modern industry – to adopt the game and push it to their zealous followers. Leagues were set up and celebrity gamers like Leo Kim and Eugene SureShot were recruited to play, making *Rolling Iron* an overnight success. But even then, only briefly. Within months interest had waned, and the ever-fickle games market had moved on, looking for the next big thing.

In Cuba, of course, things were different. Marcus had been one of the first to download a cracked copy of the RI client, and had distributed it amongst the Havana gaming community. Quickly a scene had sprung up, with hardcore gamers holding clandestine LAN parties in basements, parking lots and the backs of salsa bars. Marcus was at the centre of it all organising the get-togethers, and Paul quickly gained a reputation as the city's deadliest mech pilot. As always Marcus threw himself into customisation and hacking the game's code, pushing the experience for the thrill-starved local players. For some reason that Paul never fully understood, Marcus loved *RI* more than any other game before it, to near-obsessive levels, and mere tinkering was never enough. It was as though Marcus had to find some way of changing the game fundamentally, of making it something new, of re-inventing it as something tangibly his own.

Paul could remember the night it happened. They were sitting up on the roof of his uncle's apartment, celebrating their lance's victory over local rivals *Habaneros Mechanik* by drinking rum and sharing a stolen cigar. Marcus, however, was far from ecstatic, and instead in one of his ranting moods, complaining about how no regular, stable net access meant he couldn't easily get new levels and arenas for the game, and that without a team of artists they took too long to produce from scratch. Without new content, he said, even the desperate Havana players would lose interest soon enough, and the scene he had so lovingly nurtured would die. He was despondent.

And then – while staring out over the chaotic Havana sky-line - something must have clicked. He leaped to his feet with such force that Paul feared he would fall from the sixth storey roof to his death. It was simple, he said. He would take *Rolling Iron* to the streets.

In one of those beautiful, uncontrollable coincidences Marcus had just got hold of a crate of stolen next-gen Samsung spex from some terrifying-looking Columbian pirates. The spex were brand new, with a built-in, miniaturised brain-wave interface. Marcus' plan was simple: he'd port the *Rolling Iron* source code to the new spex, link it in with his own Havana-wide net-space, and run it as an augmented – rather than virtual - reality game.

Within two weeks Marcus had a beta client running. Paul would never forget the day he first handed him a pair of the new spex to show him it running. They had been stood not far from where they were right now, and for the first time Alphonso had appeared in real-space before him, the hairs on the back of Paul's neck standing on end as he focus-controlled him around Parque Central, weaving in and out of the locals sitting playing chess and reading their copies of Granma, total-ly oblivious to the hulking but invisible mech towering above them. It was near photo-realistic. Marcus had tweaked the ren-dering code so that the spex picked out the sun, light-sources, trees and buildings and threw accurate shadows over the ro-bot's brightly coloured metal skin. Right then, Paul somehow knew things would never be quite the same again.

Marcus named his new creation *Street Iron*, and started sell-ing the new spex pre-loaded with the client software at a knock-down price to their gaming friends in Havana. He tweaked the game rules too, to suit the tighter, faster play created by the cramped maze of Havana's streets. The mechs were now only allowed a lighter weapon load: one main range weapon – usu-ally a chain gun, a melee option and a handful of semi-guided rockets. He'd altered the shield-regeneration and gun-cooling times as well; making the combat a tense balancing match between popping from cover, waiting for your shielding to come back, watching that your weapons didn't overheat and judging when to run in for some brutal hand-to-hand combat finishes. It was a perfect piece of game-design, and proof that Marcus' skills rivalled the best that the off-island pros had to offer. Not that either of them realised anyone outside the small socialist republic would ever witness them.

Or so they thought.

Marcus was so enamoured with his work that he started to film matches, using his spex's built-in camera as well as an AR-aware handy-cam he'd managed to procure. The videos he produced were edited by a film student friend of his, with explosive results. Despite the potential repercussions if the Cuban authorities saw what he was doing, using one of his many hijacked web connections he dumped a couple of them on YouTube.

The clips - of giant mechs stomping around real-world Havana, exchanging chain gun fire and rocket attacks, clashing in ground shaking hand-to-hand combat – spread like viral wildfire around the game sites, blogs and video sharing sites. Every time he checked his YouTube page - which was infrequently due to his limited access - he seemed to have collected another hundred thousand viewers. Within weeks millions were tuning in to see what these infamous, crazy Cuban kids were doing. Comments were being left demanding to know how it was being done and where players could get hold of the software to have a go themselves. Not just that, but Paul and his lance were getting a shit-hot reputation for their *Street Iron* combat skills; *Rolling Iron* players awed at their speed and finesse on this new urban battleground.

Finally able to flaunt his coding skills to the outside world, Marcus dumped the client software – now in the form of a much more advanced, sophisticated and stable release – onto some file sharing sites. Within days it had hit half a million downloads, and blogs and forums were alight with chatter as eager hackers altered the client to run in their own locale. Less than two weeks later the videos came flooding back: clips of giant mechs clashing in the streets of London, Paris, Tokyo, Tehran, LA, Beijing, Mumbai – the major cities of the world on augmented fire as secret, unseen wars were fought. AR gaming wasn't new to the outside world; however, doing it on this kind of scale in these busy, built-up areas was usually restricted by those that provided and monitored the spex-spaces. Due to its built-from-the-ground-up, home-brew design, *Street Iron* existed outside those rules, it became something rebellious and anarchic, drawing in players desperate for a new thrill in the way no official, legitimate product ever could.

Through their illicit, ad-hoc net access Paul and Marcus watched all this unfold in quiet disbelief, fearing it was only a matter of time before what they had created came crashing down around their ears when the Cuban authorities caught wind of what they were doing. Sure enough, one day Good Cop and Bad Cop came knocking at their door. What they had to say surprised the two though. Instead of marching them off for re-education they were interested – as far as their comprehension of the technology permitted them, at least – and wanted to talk. The Cuban government had been approached by certain outside forces: Sony, Mindfield, News Corp and – perhaps most importantly – the global media and memetic powerhouse that was the gamers' guild Sakura. While the government was still reluctant to make dealings with the corrupt, imperialistic nations of the globalist northern hemisphere, it wasn't stupid enough to not talk to these independent organisations at a time of looming economic crisis. It was for the unified good of the Cuban people, Good Cop had explained, over and over again. Weeks of endless meetings and negotiations followed, until Paul and Marcus found themselves about to take the spotlight on the global stage, as Havana played host to not only the world's first official Street Iron exhibition game, but also three of the planet's most famous celebrity gamers.

"So...what d'ya think?" Marcus asked him.

Paul was still staring up at Alphonso towering above them, glistening in the ever-oppressive noon Havana sun.

"Sounds like you been busy" he replied. "Let's hope it all works."

"Only one way to find out" grinned Marcus. "Wanna take him for a spin?"

*

Paul was sat on the back of Marcus' moped as they sped through the busy noon Havana traffic, his head turned backwards watching Alphonso jogging behind them. He focus-controlled him to weave in between the oblivious road users, cursing silently to himself when he occasionally clipped a taxi or a bus.

Due to the nature of *Street Iron*'s gameplay and its huge, impromptu arenas, each player was allowed a runner with a ground-based vehicle in order to get around. Marcus was Paul's runner; his ageing but still reliable Fiat moped painted the same gleaning green and white as Alphonso. Paul felt like part of an unstoppable team every time they rode like this together. In competitions it was a pretty accurate feeling.

As they sped down towards Havana's old colonial forts and sea walls, they passed a gang of twenty or so schoolboys, presumably on their lunch break. When they spotted Paul they started whistling, whooping and shouting his name. Paul smiled and waved back timidly – this new found celebrity status a strange experience for the usually-modest young gamer. He was surprised they recognised him, but there was that short interview in the state newspaper Granma, and one of his cousins had said they'd seen his face on a billboard along the highway out towards Santa Maria del Mar.

Marcus had slowed due to traffic, and the kids were running along the pavement trying to keep level with them. Paul noticed that some of them seemed to be pointing at the space behind the moped, and he could swear that he could hear them shouting "Alphonso! Alphonso!" over the steady drone of its engine. Which was impossible, of course. Until he noticed something about the school kids. All of them.

He started tapping Marcus frantically on the shoulder.

"Pull over man! Pull over!"

"Huh?"

"Pull over!" he shouted. "Seriously!"

Marcus did as he was told, and Paul brought Alphonso to a halt behind them. Immediately the kids encircled the mech, pointing and clapping, jumping up and down and shouting in fevered excitement.

Marcus turned round to look at Paul. "What's up man? Something wrong with Alphonso?"

"Not at all. Apart from he's suddenly visible."

"What?"

They both climbed off the moped and stared in disbelief at Alphonso and the crowd of kids.

"I don't get it, what the fu-" started Marcus, and then paused as the penny dropped and the same realisation that had just hit Paul dawned on him. "They're all wearing spex!"

Marcus walked over and whipped the spex off the face of the nearest boy. They were a cheap, lightweight model, unbranded save for a small Sakura logo on each arm. He whipped his own off and put the boy's specs on instead.

"They're simple. Low res but not too bad. Better than the ones we first started with. And they're running a scaled-down, passive-spectator version of the *Street Iron* client." He looked away from Alphonso and up and down the busy Havana street. "And some other shit too. Fucking hell."

Paul bent down to talk to the eight year old. "Hey amigo, where did you get these from?" he asked him, pointing at Marcus' face.

"The Chinese." the kid said, pointing down the road. Paul squinted in the bright Cuban sun. At the quayside he could make out a large truck, the Sakura logo emblazoned on the side. Some guys in baseball caps and high-vis waistcoats were unpacking boxes and handing out their contents to the fishermen that were gathering around the truck. More free spex.

"Paul man, you really need to check this shit out." Marcus said, handing him the pair he'd taken from the boy.

Paul put them on, and had to catch his breath at what he saw.

Alphonso was there, but it was everything else that shocked him. Virtual billboards hung in the air down the street, covering the fascias of some of the buildings, or hanging across the street like banners. They were advertising games like *Rolling Iron* and *A Wind of Blades*, soft drinks and fast food, Nike shoes and other clothes. Stuff you couldn't even buy in Cuba. At least, not yet.

"Pretty fucked up, huh?" said Marcus.

Paul suddenly felt sick. He'd heard that the spex-spaces of foreign cities were like this, but somehow it didn't feel right in Havana.

"Why are they doing this?"

"It's Sakura man." Marcus replied. "They live on money and sponsorship and getting new recruits. It's what they need to survive. Hook 'em in when they're young."

"Yeah... but like this? It's too much." Paul shook his head. "It doesn't feel right."

"*Viva la Revolución*" Marcus said grimly, and climbed back onto the moped.

*

Leo Kim's lance and their various entourages had taken over the entire roof garden of the Parque Central Hotel, save for a group of bikini-wearing, giggling, shrill-voiced but vacant looking air hostesses that had been allowed into the pre-party for some much-needed female presence. The air was full of the smell of barbecued meat and Latin-tinged house music, as swallows swooped low across the pool to grab beak-fulls of the chlorinated water.

Paul had passed the hotel almost every day of his life, but until now the closest he'd got to entering was being moved along for loitering by the heavily armed security. It wasn't a place for locals, but today he and his lance were the guests of Sakura.

His two wingmen, Enrique and Alejandro, were already getting stuck in to the free buffet, while Marcus was absorbed behind his spex, lost in the thrill of free, fast net access. Paul, though, felt out of place, and had drifted away from the crowd, leaning against the railing. He stared across at the impressive view of the decaying, chaotic barrios and out to the blue Atlantic Ocean beyond.

"Feels kinda wrong, don't it?" a voice said to his right. He couldn't quite place the accent, but he guessed it was English. He turned to see a tired, sunburnt foreigner in scruffy shorts and t-shirt grasping a bottle of beer. Definitely English.

"How do you mean?" he replied.

"Sitting here, amongst all this opulence, looking out at all that poverty" the man replied, taking a swig of his drink.

Paul smiled back at him. "That poverty is where I live."

The man looked startled. "Shit, sorry mate. I meant no offence, really - "

"None taken. Really. I think you're probably quite right."

The man extended a slightly sweaty hand. "I'm John. John Smith. You're Paul Escobar, right? The *Street Iron* legend? Nice to meet you."

"And you." Paul said, shaking his hand. "What brings you to Havana, John? Are you with Sakura?"

"Yeah, for my sins." He chuckled mysteriously. "Quite literally, in fact. I'm Leo Kim's personal documentary film-maker. Means I follow him around everywhere, giving him a reach-around as I do. The fucking prick."

Paul's spex were struggling with translating the Englishman's accent and vocabulary, but he was getting the gist. He liked the guy's attitude already.

"So have you met his lance yet?" Smith continued.

"Can't say I have."

"Well, the ice maiden over there is Mako Kobiyashi" he said, pointing at a tiny Japanese girl hiding under an enormous parasol in the corner, wearing something that Paul thought was either a bondage-bikini or lolicon cosplay. "She's the archetypal spoilt Japanese princess. Comes from pure Zaibatsu stock. Doesn't really talk to anyone, but be careful. She's a crafty little witch."

"Thanks for the advice."

"And you see that Aryan-looking motherfucker in the hot tub with the trolley-dollies? Mikhail Ivanovich. His family controls most of the natural gas resources in the Balkans. Piss his dad off and all of Europe gets plunged into icy darkness. Also: he's an arrogant cunt."

Paul laughed. "And Leo Kim? He's not here yet?"

"Nah." snorted Smith. "And I wouldn't expect him to put in an appearance any time soon. Fucking weirdo is sat down in his room right now jacked into his fantasy castle, probably rubbing himself off over his non-existent sword collection or trying to hump that unicorn of his. Jesus Christ. But you've met him before, right?"

"Only in Third Person." Paul replied.

"Yeah, well my advice is, do yerself a favour and keep it that way as long as you can." Smith answered. "The guy ain't right."

"What about the others?" Paul asked him, looking around. "I should probably go introduce myself?"

"Nah. Fuck 'em. Really, you're not missing out. Leave it

for the battlefield tomorrow. And truthfully, whether I work for Sakura or not, I hope your boys give them a fucking good kicking. All three of them deserve nothing more than bloody noses. Now c'mon, let me get you a drink."

*

Paul left the party early, and as soon as he got out of the cab at his uncle's building, Mama Julia started shouting at him.

The huge, dark-skinned woman and her pack of near-feral children lived two floors down from Paul and his uncle, and she pointed at him with one of her oversized, flickering OLED-encrusted fake nails.

"You'd better get your ass upstairs" she boomed at him, absent-mindedly clipping the ear of one of the kids running round her wide legs. "Your uncle is looking for you, and he don't look happy."

Paul was a little drunk, but the ascent up the wooden stairwell – carefully stepping over the gaps where he had memorised the boards had rotted through – always forced him to sober up. When he reached their tiny, hot apartment Uncle Jose was staring silently out of one of the open windows, through a pair of the free Sakura spex.

As Paul entered his uncle turned to face him, throwing the spex down onto the table with some tangible disgust.

Jose had once been a successful academic, teaching history at Havana University, but the man gave it up when Paul's father died to raise him and his sister. With his responsibilities, Jose never married, not having a chance to meet someone. Paul understood the sacrifices he had made for him, and seeing him visibly upset now struck Paul like a fist.

The elderly man lowered his greying head and rubbed his temples as he finally spoke. "Paul, I know the Party is behind your deal with these Sakura people, but tell me, what do you think? Do you think they really have Cuba's best interests at heart?"

Paul was stunned by his uncle's words. Jose had been a life-long party loyalist, and to hear him even questioning its judgement was unheard of. He was old enough to remember the dark times of the last century, the days of grapefruit skin steaks and eighteen-hour power cuts, and he would lecture Paul and his sister about how it was the Party that had made the tough decisions that helped Cuba to survive. Paul was unsure what to say to him.

"I think, Uncle, they mainly have their own interests at heart." he said, cautiously. "But the Party thinks they will bring changes – and money and technology – that will help Cuba."

"I see." Jose raised his head to look at him, and Paul was surprised and relived to see just a glimmer of reassurance flicker across the old man's face. "You know I trust your judgement Paul. I just hope you are making the right choice. Not just for Cuba, but for yourself. Make sure you are becoming what you want to be, not just some foolish, toy-selling children's entertainer."

And with that, he turned and looked back out of the window. Paul watched him for a while, in silence, not knowing what to do or say.

*

Central Havana was gripped by a carnival vibe the morning of the match. Half the population seemed to be out in the streets; local bands played salsa beats while hustlers worked the crowds selling cigars, mojitos and pork sandwiches. Foreign and state TV crews were set up on street corners, and tiny News Corp UAVs buzzed fly-like between the ornate, pastel-coloured buildings. Sakura had set up a handful of large OLED screens around the three mile square area which had been designated the playing-field, and totally closed to conventional traffic, but from what Paul could see most of the spectators already had a pair of the free, dumbed-down spex.

Usually before a game Paul was hyped and eager to fight, but the crowds made him nervous. *Street Iron* had never been a spectator sport for him, in fact quite the opposite: it was a secret, covert activity, matches shared between a select knowing few, even when played out in the most public of spaces. He knew these streets like the back of his hand, and had done so for years, but somehow the presence of the crowd changed the layout. He'd have to ignore them as usual, but was worried that their being able to see him and react would make that harder to do. It was as if the watching masses were a new, unpredictable and unwanted force in this world that he and Marcus had created. Certainly seeing the kids react to Alphonso the other day had freaked him out, and he felt truly outside his comfort zone.

Sitting on the back of Marcus' freshly waxed moped, he closed his eyes and took a deep breath, desperately trying to block out the surrounding crowd's chants, shouts and whistles of support; and the ever-present sound of drumming. To either side, both Alejandro and Enrique were also preparing themselves, although both them and their runners seemed more relaxed - Enrique in particular soaking up the attention, even waving and shouting back. Enjoy it, thought Paul, but stay frosty.

Enrique's runner was his cousin Fredo, and as such had the most glamorous of rides – Fredo's 1955 black and white Pontiac convertible. Alejandro on the other hand had lucked-out, having to settle instead with his brother and his tiny, pod-like three-wheeled coco-bean taxi. Paul smiled when he glanced over at it; he knew Alejandro was embarrassed to be being seen across the globe riding the weird little bright yellow cab, but it was such a uniquely Cuban image that it made him feel a certain kind of pride.

In front of each of them, in the space cordoned off from the crowd, stood their mechs - all systems online and ready for combat.

As the clock in the top left of his vision hit noon, the sky above Havana was filled with numbers, and the game-start countdown began. The crowd noise suddenly hit a new level, and Paul felt his guts tighten. He knew their support was fully behind him, but in all honesty he wished they would just shut up. He only hoped that across the other side of the arena the Sakura All-Star players were getting as much shit as he was getting love. Knowing Habaneros, he was pretty sure they were.

The counter hit zero, the crowd hit fever pitch, the hunt was on. All three of them pulled away, their mechs running in front of them, with his two wingmen veering off to his left and right, disappearing into the maze-like side streets to take up their standard flanking positions. If the Cubans had one advantage it was their inch-perfect knowledge of the playing field, and despite however many Google Earth simulations Kim's teams must have run he was convinced it would give them the edge.

As he and Marcus powered towards Parque Central – this time with Alphonso running in front of the bike for maximum visibility – Paul was surprised to hear the synthetic booming of chain gun fire from his right. Enrique had already entered combat. The spex-wearing crowd heard it too, turning and running into the side streets like stampeding cattle to get their first glimpse of action.

"Enrique?" he shouted into his com-link.

"The Japanese girl." he came back instantly, "She's on me." His voice was nearly drowned out by the roar of heavy weapon fire.

Paul made a snap tactical decision to back him up, turning the sprinting Alphonso down a side alley between crumbling tenements, excited onlookers screaming support from balconies and the lampposts they'd climbed to get a better view. It was distracting, and Paul was already starting to doubt his own decision-making, worried he was being spurred on by the desires of the baying crowd.

Paul and Marcus followed Alphonso into the tight space of Plaza del Cristo, but it was clear it was too late. The smouldering hulk of Enrique's Triumph-class mech lay in a heap at one end of the square, and the flustered looking wingman had leapt from the Pontiac and was running over the cobbled ground towards the moped, waving his arms in the air. When your mech died so did your com-link, and the wingman was desperately trying to shout something over the roar of the crowd and the clanking of Alphonso's huge metal feet on the stones, but all Paul could make out was something about 'jumping'. He didn't have time to listen though, as Mako's pink, Hello Kitty-festooned *Raptor*-class mech was anxiously trying to back away out of the square. From the steam rising from the mech's gauss cannon and the speed at which the Japanese girl was trying to make it flee Paul guessed both its weapons and shields needed time to cool and recharge. Enrique must have put up a good fight.

The disorientated Mako had backed her brightly-coloured machine into a cul-de-sac, and let off the last two of her rockets, the deadly projectiles screaming across the plaza leaving anime-style contrails behind them, but Alphonso was too quick, Paul too focused. The green and white mech skilfully swerved past them, returning fire with three of its own rockets. All three of the rockets hit home, Paul finishing off the kill with a burst of chain gun fire. The childish-looking mech was hurled back by repeated impacts, falling upon the surrounding crowd, who instinctively scattered from the perceived danger of the artificial falling metal carcass.

First kill for Cuba. The audience whooped and screamed with delight, and out of the corner of his eye Paul spotted a tantrum-throwing Mako in the far corner of the plaza, slamming her fists on the rear seat of her open top Sakura Hum-Vee, and chastising her driver. Paul allowed himself a quick smile, but there was no time to celebrate. The whistle of rockets and the jarring pounding of cannon fire was echoing from the direction of the Capital building.

When he got there, Alejandro's camouflage-painted *Puma-V* and Ivanovich's battleship-grey *Predator* were duelling in the surrounding grounds, dodging around palm trees and letting off short bursts of chain gun fire, rocket-contrails still hanging in the air. Paul instinctively held Alphonso back; partly to check his temperature and shields, but mainly to let Alejandro go for the kill. Despite the ribbing he got for his unconventional runner's ride, the young Cuban was an adept pilot, fast and focused, and probably second only to Paul himself on the island. Plus time and time again he had shown himself to have a few tricks up his sleeve.

He was about to do it again. Getting in close to the Russian – too close, it seemed – he faked a misfire, discharging his chain gun wide of the mark. The *Predator* paused to unleash its remaining rockets, but Alejandro sent his mech downwards into a dive to the ground, falling into an elaborate, impossible looking Capoeira move - spinning the heavy machinery on its shoulders and sweep-kicking the Russian's legs from under it, before jumping back upright. It was breathtaking, and Paul couldn't help but laugh at the pilot's audacity.

The *Predator* hit the ground with an ear-ringing thud, its shields drained by the impact, facing the wrong end of Alejandro's chain gun at point blank range as it struggled to get up. Second kill for the Cubans. The crowd hit fever pitch once more.

As Paul broke cover, congratulating Alejandro on the kill, something moved in the periphery of his vision. Something large, and impossibly high up. Leo Kim's mech emerged from behind the vast dome of the Capitol building, teetering on the edge of the ageing but beautiful structure.

How the fuck did he get it up there? Paul thought, but he didn't have time for answer. In a blur of Sakura colours the mech leapt; Kim's trademarked, oversized plasma-edged katana held high, the blade making contact with Alejandro's mech's shoulder as he landed.

With the *Puma-V's* shields still recharging and the force of Kim's deafening landing behind it the sword met little resistance, cleaving straight through the mech's torso. There was a second's pause, an over-the-top anime kachiinnnk sound effect, then *Puma-V* fell, in two halves.

Paul got his first proper, in-person look at Kim's mech. It was based on a *Hellcat* model identical to Alphonso, but it had undergone similar stylistic and performance modifications, making the two seem like totally different machines at a first, uneducated glance. The body armour had been painted with bright purples and reds, and was dotted with stylised, white – almost snowflake-like – cherry blossoms, mimicking Kim's iconic kimono from *A Wind of Blades*, the online game-come-soap opera that he was still best known for. But it was the deadly, glowing katana that held Paul's main attention. The Cubans had always shunned the option of equipping their mechs with melee weapons – trading off a lighter and thus faster machine against their love for unarmed, hand-to-hand combat – but Paul was starting to wonder for the first time if this had been a wise choice.

He only allowed himself nanoseconds to contemplate it, and then he was moving again, firing.

The crowd had fallen silent, shocked by Alejandro's sudden slaying, but burst into noise once more as they saw Paul respond. Alphonso hailed chain gun fire upon the Korean, but Kim was too quick, the shells slamming into the Capitol building, leaving a trail of metre-wide, cartoon-like fake bullet holes across the colonial façade.

The two players fell instinctively into standard one-on-one duel tactics; moving from cover point to cover point, popping out to chip away at each other's shields with cannon fire or the occasional well-aimed rocket.

Paul felt uncomfortable. Something wasn't right, his focus slipping. It was the crowds again, they were both distracting him and influencing his decision-making, their baying for blood subconsciously forcing him to edge Alphonso ever closer to Kim's *Hellcat*, to take greater risks. Alert windows filled the augmented space around his head; temperature gauges and shield levels flashing into the red. Whether his choice or the crowd's, he would have to finish it now.

Kim had been wielding the oversized katana as a body shield to deflect some of Paul's chain gun fire away from the mech's torso. It still counted as hits against the shield, but the amount of depletion was lessened: a tactic popularised by Kim, but requiring greater skill and focus than the average player could command. It was tricky even for Kim, and occasionally Paul noticed that that the attempts to parry the shots would actually leave him more exposed, as the player misjudged when to let shots just go naturally wide of target.

Paul started to work it, finding he could trick the flamboyant, showboating pro into parrying misfired shots and leaving him exposed. He got in close, dodging Kim's last rocket while firing the chain gun deliberately wide, Kim's insistence on deflecting the rounds leaving him temporarily exposed.

Paul pushed Alphonso downwards and into a charge, knowing he had the timing millisecond-perfect. A shoulder barge while the Korean was prone would leave the mech sprawled on the mangled, concrete Havana streets, and a follow up curbstomp to the skull would mean game over.

Kim's reaction as Alphonso charged almost made Paul laugh at first. The Korean had seemed to panic, making the mech jump on the spot – and as fast and acrobatic as the Street Iron units were, even under the control of the most adept pilots they couldn't leap straight up more than a few metres. They were too heavy, and even Marcus' tweaked physics engine wouldn't allow it.

Except that was seemingly exactly what Leo Kim was now making his *Hellcat* do.

Paul's amusement turned to stunned disbelief. Kim's mech was hanging in the air, hovering on thrusts of blue flame and steam from its over-sized feet, as uncaring momentum ploughed Alphonso headfirst through now empty space and into the ground. Paul struggled to right the mech, shields gone as it rolled in clouds of simulated dust, but all he could do was watch the Korean mech fall from the sky as quick as it had risen.

The glowing plasma edge of the katana cut silently through Alphonso's unshielded metal skin, piercing the mech's reactor-heart. Blue lighting lit the dust cloud, arcing out into the Havana sky as Kim withdrew the sword and stepped back from the inevitable: the sunburst explosion that had every watching spectator trying to shield their spex-covered eyes.

Paul gripped Marcus' shoulders, his legs weak with shock and his throat dry, as the sky over Havana filled with the words GAME OVER.

*

Paul and his lance were sat in the back of a noisy, smoke-filled bar in Vieja, waiting for the rum to kick in and numb the pain.

Around them Havana drank and danced, never a city to pass up an excuse to party. The atmosphere had been muted for a while after the match, but if Cubans had taught themselves one thing over the last seventy five years, it was how to drown their sorrows.

Sadly for Paul it wasn't working; the alcohol unable to penetrate the thick shield of anger that surrounded him. Even though he'd removed his spex hours ago, he felt removed and displaced from everything in his proximity, as though the augmented illusion was in the reality around him . He hadn't spoke for hours, not to the passers-by that had commiserated him with slaps on the back, not to the waiters that had brought free glass after free glass of rum, and not even to Good Cop when he appeared, dishing out expensive cigars, all grins and hand-shakes, talking about how well they'd played in spite of the odds, how Cuba was proud of them, and how today would be remembered as an important day in the nation's great history.

Which was why Marcus had almost jumped out of his skin when Paul did finally speak.

"They fucking cheated" he said.

"Well..." Marcus shrugged. "We been discussing it man, technically if they had -"

"Net connection." Paul muttered.

"What?" Marcus said, leaning in to hear Paul over the roar of the busy bar.

"Net connection." he replied, more clearly. "Can you get me a net connection?"

*

"Paul, thanks for the visit." Leo Kim said dryly. "I was planning on contacting you in the morning, as it happens."

His throne room was obsidian-dark, the only light source a single shaft from above, that reflected off the scales of the two huge Komodo dragons that eyed Paul lazily from around Kim's feet.

"You cheated" Paul said.

Kim sighed. "You're referring to the jump-jets I assume? It's a shame you feel that way. They were included in the last upgrade to the Sakura-approved client last month. Of course we should have realised the problems you have getting updates here."

"Marcus writes the client. He makes the rules."

"Not any more, I'm afraid. I'm sure there'll be a role for him as an advisor to Mindfield, I'll make sure of it person-ally. He'll be very well rewarded. As will you. Which is what I wanted to talk to you about.

"Join my lance, Paul. I'm tired of the German, his attitude bores me and he's losing focus. The trappings of celebrity too easily distract him. You seem more… down to earth. Grounded. Join Sakura and we'll get you off this island."

It felt like the air around Paul's head had frozen, solidified.

Everything he and Marcus had talked about, being handed to him on a plate.

"Okay." Paul said, dry mouthed. "On one condition. Beat me again."

"Sorry?"

"I want a rematch." Paul said, as sternly as he could manage. "One-on-one. Tomorrow. Beat me again and I'll sign anything you want."

"Seriously?" Kim grinned, Paul unsure if it was a sign of amusement or surprised gamer respect. "And if I don't win? Then what?"

"Then you fuck off out of Cuba. You and Sakura. Permanently."

Kim laughed. "Really? I don't think your government would approve of that."

"That's for me to worry about." he bluffed.

"And you? You'd seriously throw this all away, to defend some broken pride?"

It was more than that, Paul knew, but he felt no responsibility to explain it to Kim. "Find out tomorrow, when you try and beat me."

The Korean paused before he spoke. "Okay. If it'll make you happy. Where and when?"

"I'll mail you details shortly." Paul replied. "And one more thing. This is a private match. No spectators. No crowds. No media. Just you and me. This is private. Understand?"

Kim grinned again. "Of course."

Paul ported out.

*

Somewhere out in the Florida Straits an unborn hurricane

94

was dying; its failed energy lashing Havana with warm fingers of wind that rattled palms and whistled through derelict windows.

On Paul's insistence Kim had ditched the Sakura Hummer in an attempt to avoid drawing attention. Instead he sat in the rear of Fredo's 1955 black and white Pontiac convertible, Enrique's cousin had taken some convincing to part with his pride and joy, and had lectured Kim's runner for near to an hour about the machine's handling and eccentricities. Paul had felt sorry for the guy; obviously excited at getting his hands on the beast when he'd first arrived to pick it up, he'd left looking baffled and scared for his life, gingerly pulling out into the hectic Havana traffic while a fretting and fidgeting Fredo watched on, shaking his head.

Kim hadn't been there, of course. Peering at him now from the opposite side of Parque Central, Paul realised it was only the second time he'd seen him in the flesh. The last time had been just after the demonstration match had ended, as his Hummer had sped Kim back to the air-conditioned sanctuary of the hotel. Both times, his face had been hidden by his tinted LG spex and anti-pandemic surgical mask, making Paul recall the stories he'd heard that he was a hygiene-obsessed, germ phobic recluse. Paul pushed it out of his mind, along with the stories he'd heard from Smith: past failures had taught him the importance of not allowing perceived weaknesses to cause him to underestimate an opponent. For all the net rumours and media mythology surrounding Kim, Paul knew that behind all the market manipulation, hype and viral spin there was a reason the Korean was considered the best pro-gamer in the world.

He glanced up at Alphonso next to him, the mech still battered and war-scarred from yesterday's defeat. Although each mech started a fresh game at its full capability, Marcus had tweaked the *Street Iron* engine so that it took several wins for the visual scars to fade. On the street - he'd proudly announced, like he was the voiceover man for a game trailer – you're only as good as your last fight.

Once again, the sky over Havana filled with numbers. Paul grasped Marcus' shoulders tightly, feeling his friend's body tense up as he leant forwards on the bike.

At zero they were moving, the two mechs circling each other, chain gun fire raining spent cartridges down onto the oblivious residents that milled around their feet. Again, almost in a replay of their last clash, the two pilots pushed their mechs closer to each other. Impatience had been Paul's downfall then, but as though stubbornly refusing to take his lesson he forced Alphonso forward, filling the air between the two with rocket contrails and gunfire. By contrast, Kim seemed to have taken his mistakes on board, rolling with the hits and parrying only those he safely could, rather than unwittingly exposing himself again. It was wise, but it meant Paul was pushing him back towards the walls of the capital building, denying him space to move.

In fact, Paul realised, something seemed askew with the Korean's playing style. He seemed far more reserved, lacking in confidence, all his usual flamboyancy missing. And then it struck him; the crowds were gone. While they had been a crippling distraction for the young Cuban, for Kim they were his lifeblood, their noise and energy not just fuelling his adrenaline but defining who he was. Even the Havana crowds, which had screamed hatred at him and bayed for his blood, without their mere presence, he must have felt alone, pointless. A celebrity performer denied attention, adoring or despising, was nothing.

Feeling confident, Paul pushed forward again, getting dangerously close to the plasma katana's striking range. Before Kim could swing though, he unleashed the last of Alphonso's rockets – the impact at this range would be devastating, wiping the mech's shields dead. But Paul guessed what was coming.

The Korean *Hellcat* jumped, jets igniting below its feet.

"Punch it!" Paul screamed in Marcus' ear.

The coder stabbed a floating, translucent window he'd positioned just above his right handlebar, his finger penetrating right through the 'run' button, expanding concentric circles rippling across the custom script launcher.

The game-world froze. Paul had seen it happen before, especially in the early *Street Iron* days, when Marcus' clients had been far less stable, but it never ceased to fascinate him. It was a jarring but somehow beautiful experience, suddenly being reminded that what you were focused upon was just an illusion, paused, as the real world – the actual reality – carried on oblivious around you. The two mechs were silent, motionless statues, rockets and chain gun rounds hanging unrealistically in the air. For a brief second Paul was out of the game again, taking nanoseconds to glance around him at Havana   - the people, the architecture. Just there, in the depth of the deliberate software glitch, what he was doing finally made sense.

Kim's mech hung in the air, and when the script had run its cycle, and everything came back to screaming, full volume life, its jump jets were gone, removed from non-existence by Marcus' roll-back patch. Falling to the ground with the elegance of scrap-metal, it took the brunt of most of Paul's rockets on the way down.

The Hellcat sprawled on the broken Havana pavement, shields wiped. Alphonso towered above, the end of his chain gun mere feet from the prone mech's skull. For an instant, Paul hesitated.

The instant became longer.

Marcus looked back over his shoulder. "What the fuck man? Finish him!"

"Too easy," Paul murmured.

Leo Kim was fast. In one move he not only flicked the Hellcat up from its prone position, but used the momentum to swing his katana hard into Alphonso's stationary frame. Blue lightening arched across the two metal giants as the plasma blade shorted out shields, red warning icons flashing all around

Paul's face. He grasped Marcus' shoulders once more.

"Run" he said, loudly.

He spun Alphonso round and over their heads, the vulnerable mech sprinting away from the busy square, and Marcus wheeling the bike round to follow it. Before Paul knew it they were hurtling down Paseo de Marti into oncoming traffic, Alphonso ahead of them, closely followed by Kim's *Hellcat*. Above the honks and screams of the confused traffic Paul swore he could make out the distinctive purr of Fredo's Pontiac, and glancing to his left there it was, Leo Kim sat in the back seat, his mask gone now and a shit-eating grin spreading across his face. He was back, the Kim of legend, the unpredictable thrill of the fight substitution enough for the lack of attention. It was, thought Paul, the first time he'd seen him looking like he was having fun.

Maybe, he thought, he should have ended this when he'd had the fucking chance.

As Alphonso reached the end of the road, Paul jumped him off the sea wall, the huge mechs soaring above the oblivious heads of the young couples and scruffy anglers that were perched along it. Marcus skidded the bike to a sideways halt, Kim's nervous runner doing similar with Fredo's treasured ride, as Alphonso crashed into the sea, spraying fountains of synthetic water into the evening sky. Paul spun him round, waist deep in the ocean, and opened fire with the chain gun. Kim's mech had already entered the water behind him, and he didn't slow his charge, taking the bombardment full on, knowing Paul couldn't sustain the burst for long. Sure enough, within seconds temperature alerts flashed red across his whole periphery, and the gun fell silent.

Seeing his chance, Kim unleashed his remaining rockets.

And Alphonso crouched.

The massive mech vanished beneath the waves, a plume of steam from its overheating frame sizzling into the air.

Within a second of being in the cool water the temperature

gauges had flipped back to green, as Kim's rockets arched lazily and pointlessly into the sea.

Alphonso popped up again, chain gun whirring, its oversized shells ripping through what was left of Kim's shields and tearing apart the metal beneath as if it was paper. One round knocked the skull into a sickening, disjointed angle, while two others shattered the katana blade, the rest pummelling and shredding the chest armour, exposing the reactor.

The fusion-blast lit Havana for miles, though only four men saw it, as they struggled to rip the spex from their faces before it temporarily whited-out their retinas.

Paul looked over at Kim, his face exposed fully for the first time. The Korean looked stunned, but not distraught. He looked, to Paul, too exhilarated for that.

And no one in Havana saw the words GAME OVER fill the sky.

*

"I'm sorry man," Paul said quietly. "I've fucked everything up."

"Shut up, man." Marcus replied.

The were sat up on Uncle Jose's roof once again, listening to sounds of salsa and sirens drift across the cityscape.

Sakura had already left the island. Kim, out of respect for Paul, had made up some bullshit excuse for the whole deal falling through, letting him off the hook with the government. They got away with it, but all Paul felt was guilt, and the dull, irritating pain of missed opportunities.

"You didn't fuck anything up." Marcus continued. "You did Cuba a fucking favour. We both did. You saw what they would have turned this place into. Just like everywhere fucking else they go. It wasn't right."

"Yeah, but what about you man? They would have given you a job. Just like you- "

"What? You think I would have wanted to work for them?" Marcus shook his head. "Nah, man. No way. You did me a favour too. And I realise exactly what I want- "

Marcus was interrupted by a commotion in the street below, both of them carefully leaning forward on the rickety roof to see what was going on.

A cab had screeched to a halt, and a small child – one of Mama Julia's boys, it looked like – had leaped out of the back. He was yelling Paul's name, and waving what looked like an envelope above his head.

Marcus sighed loudly. "Now what?"

*

They met the kid halfway down the rotting, wooden stairs. He was red-faced and out of breath, and the only word he seemed able to say was 'English'.

Paul took the package from him, and ripped it open. Inside was a messy handwritten note on Hotel Parque Central headed paper, with a wafer-thin 32TB memory stick paper-clipped to the top left corner. He plucked it off and handed it to Marcus, who leaned in close to read the note over his shoulder.

The handwriting was scruffy, and at first his spex struggled to translate the English text.

Paul! Hope you are cool.

Last night was special man. Wow.

And guess what? Yeah. I filmed the whole thing.

I think the whole world should see it, but I figured if it were to get released, we'd BOTH be in the complete shit. Me, I'll be fine. I got a server in Dubai so full of weirdness about Kim that he

wouldn't dare lay a finger on me. But not sure how your government would react, so I'm leaving the decision up to you.

Good meeting you man. Hope we'll run into each other again. You owe me a drink for a start.

Adios amigo,
John Smith.

Paul turned to Marcus, who held the memory stick up in front of his face.

"So? What you gonna do?"

Paul thought for a second, and then grinned at his friend.

"Can you get me a net connection?"

*

Paul squinted in the midday sun as they opened the gate and let him out of the CDR re-education centre.

The six weeks he'd spent in there hadn't been anywhere near as bad as he'd feared. The food was pretty good for a start, and the rest of the inmates friendly enough, especially after they found out who he was. Somehow even the prisoners who were in there for long stretches had seen the footage. And even the four hours a day of old Castro speeches wasn't too hard to take, given all the chocolate and rum that the guards used to slip him. One day even Bad Cop had come to visit him, bringing him some cigars and illegal US comics that had obviously been seized off some other poor geek. As usual he didn't say much, apart from asking him to sign a picture of Alphonso for his son.

Still, it was good to get out, and seeing Marcus sitting on his bike on the other side of the road waiting for him was even better.

The two friends embraced, Marcus pulling away to look Paul up and down.

"They treat you alright man?"

"Yeah, it was okay. And you?"

Marcus grinned. "Amigo. I was only in there two weeks. Then they took me out."

Paul was confused. "What? Where did they take you?"

"The university. I've been in a software lab up there for the last month. You won't believe the shit I've been doing. We're going legit man."

"Legit?"

"Si. My network, the spex spaces – it's all going legal. The government is funding me to upgrade it all, buying me new wireless gear and everything. At first it was just going to be for tourists, but I managed to convince them to take it further. All those spex Sakura gave away – well, they couldn't take them back, so they shut them down remotely. Bricked 'em. But they forgot about Marcus, right?

"I wrote a patch – it's a virus, really – that flashes them, reboots them and installs my own software on them. We've infected the whole network with it. Thousands of people across Havana have suddenly got a working pair of spex, and are using them every day."

Paul couldn't quite believe what he was hearing. "Don't bullshit me- "

"No bullshit man. See for yourself."

Marcus reached inside a pocket and handed Paul a pair of spex. He recognised them straight away as the cheaply-made ones that Sakura had been handing out, except that their logo had been scratched off the arms and replaced with a tiny sticker of the Cuban flag. Paul slipped them onto his face.

And suddenly Alphonso was there; towering above them in the bright, hot Cuban sun.

He looked more magnificent than Paul remembered ever seeing him before. Not only had all his battle scars gone, but